By Fielding Dawson

Stories & Dreams:

Krazy Kat/The Unveiling
The Dream/Thunder Road
The Sun Rises Into The Sky
The Man Who Changed Overnight

Novels:

Open Road
The Mandalay Dream
A *Great* Day for a Ballgame
Penny Lane
Two Penny Lane

Novellas:

Elizabeth Constantine
Thread
The Greatest Story Ever Told/A Transformation

Memoirs:

An Emotional Memoir of Franz Kline
The Black Mountain Book (A memoir of the college)

Essays & Criticism:

An Essay on New American Fiction
Entelechy One

PENNY LANE

A NOVEL

FIELDING DAWSON

SANTA BARBARA
BLACK SPARROW PRESS
1977

LIBRARY OF CONGRESS CATALOGING IN PUBLICATION DATA

Dawson, Fielding, 1930-
  Penny Lane : a novel.

  I. Title.
PZ4.D27235Pe [PS3554.A948]   813'.5'4   77-11690
ISBN 0-87685-315-7
ISBN 0-87685-314-9 pbk.

For Jamie

"Our datum is the actual world, including ourselves; and this actual world spreads itself for observation in the guise of the topic of our immediate experience. The elucidation of immediate experience is the sole justification for any thought; and the starting point for any thought is the analytic observation of components of this experience."

—Whitehead
Process and Reality

"But—"
"But me no buts," I said.

—Chandler
Farewell, My Lovely

Table of Contents

PENNY LANE

Prologue

TWA Met. Flight 171 Home

What will you do? they asked.

Keep on until it changes, he answered, and put a little salt and pepper on his stuffed tomato. The two brothers looked across the table at him.

Dave, the oldest, smiled, and said Yes, but what will you do when she's gone?

That's a problem, he admitted.

They looked at each other, and grinned: get him, they said. A problem. How about the money angle, Dave said.

That's another problem, he admitted.

How does she feel about it? Herb asked.

She's worried.

The waitress appeared, a typical small town woman in her late twenties, with a pale face, bad legs and big grin. "Everything okay?" she cried, gaily.

They grinned, and nodded, yes, sure.

Really?

Really.

Well listen, Herb said, and slapped me on the back: Good luck. I hope you know what you're doing!

Then, like his father before him, he made a sly smile, and asked, Do you?

No, I said. But I'll sure as hell find out.

He knows what he's doing, Dave said, he just can't say it.

We left the restaurant.

The Ohio sun poured down on us as we walked along toward their office. The old sandstone train station across the two way traffic seemed to bleach in the heat.

I shook hands with them, and said so long.

Where are you going from here? Dave asked.

Lansing, I said. My son's just graduated from high school—

I knew that the children from both of their marriages were in college. Also, that Dave and his wife had split up.

We said so long, old childhood friends that we were, and after shaking hands, they went inside the building. I stood on the street in the sun, wondering. Then I turned, and went back inside the restaurant to the bar.

The bartender's name was Jim, and he grinned hello. He reached across and we shook hands as I sat down.

The bar was empty.

And bland. Very bland.

The usual? Jim asked.

I smiled, and nodded yes, thinking that in just three days he had gotten to know what the usual was.

I walked up Main Street feeling like the third person, passing the old familiar places and sights from my childhood. I crossed my old grade school playground, deserted in summer vacation. The asphalt was tacky in the heat, and when I got home I'd pick tar and pebbles off the soles of my shoes. I walked vast, feeling numb from the drinks, and the horizontal small town's transparency, shimmering in the heat. That's what that is, and why one of the women in the office where Dave and Herb worked had said nobody says hello to strangers on the streets anymore.

He nodded, truly, I thought, it didn't make any difference. Although it did, and so much.

Friday, and transparent.

I was glad the heat was on.

I sat on my bed in my childhood room and picked tar and pebbles off the soles of my shoes, as I sipped the usual, ice cold. The room was cool in the breeze, and the crabapple tree outside my window, plus my childhood books by my bed made me sentimental, and rather happy. My uncle had come out of the coma and was demanding cigarettes from adamant nurses—he won't die, and his wife, my aunt, was home from the cross-county hospital where she'd been, shock had worked, and she was much better: normal, in lively good spirits. My mother was glad I'd come home, and we had good long talks. On the front porch, in the evenings, as a few of the vanishing fireflies returned to our yard, to remind me.

Later, up the street.

There were a few of these Americans left. Not many, but a few. The kind of person who would, from across the street, wave and call a natural good morning, to a stranger.

We were in her living room, drinking the usual.

I talked about transparency. Small towns were horizontal, silent, and transparent. Bland, and shimmering from the surface up.

But the jungle and the desert were vertical, and deep in their certain tonal vision, and—

That, she gently admonished me, is an abstract opinion, which I'm not sure I understand.

That's you and me both, I said, feeling less like the third person than before, though a little, still.

The man in his mid-forties and the woman in her late sixties went outside and sat on pillows in wooden chairs in the darkness, and talked, and sipped their drinks. The stars were out. It wasn't so hot as it had been, and there was a cool breeze. I told her the good news of my family, and she said Your mother must be proud.

I nodded.

Me too, I thought.

So are you, she smiled, in the darkness.

It was late when I got home. I went in the kitchen, opened the refrigerator and made myself the usual, but unusually tough, and with it I went outside and across the lawn into the side yard by the sundial, and in almost pitch darkness, I stripped, and stretched out on the chilled dewy grass. Except for the white across my thighs, I was tan, and I blended in and looked up at the stars, and listened to the night cries, and watched the fireflies flashing in their appointed territories.

I closed my eyes. I slept a little.

I woke and rose on my right elbow, and sipped my drink.

I gazed across the lawn, and fell into a reflective mood. Before I'd come home I had finished the first draft on a novel, in just six weeks. Brand new work. I was pleased, and unusually enthusiastic with it.

With hard work the final draft would be done in a month.

I sipped, and again lay back. I looked up at the stars. My novel concluded in a magic change.

Tomorrow I would fly to Lansing, see my son Jamie, to whom I had dedicated the novel. For his highschool graduation present, and into the future for him to look back on.

As we got to know each other.

Shortly before I'd gotten the urgent come-home call from Mother (although I knew—had known—I was going home, and that my uncle was seriously ill) my novel had fallen together into completion, and in the deep fulfillment I had had a dream that night, from which I woke, mystified, delighted, and in awe.

Walking. Walking as I had through my life across fields, highways, mountains and over bridges, I walked through fields until I went off the road into an orchard, and having passed through it, I emerged upon a sloping green hill.

I walked up it as I thought I would descend the other side, not minding it, for I felt enchanted, and yet not comprehending where-I-was, as it was familiar and not. It was strange.

I reached the crest of the hill to find a higher hill before me, yet sloping off and up to my right with a sort of valley below where I saw several cottages, scattered like in summer camp, and as I walked into the valley I was uphill, for the ground was firm, and the figures I saw who seemed to be curiously wrestling, or gripping each other, were ahead of me, and rather unwillingly, but accepting my step, I went toward them.

The figures were as the cottages, placed at random, and in fact seeming as statues, and there were as many statues as cottages, though not meaning there was a statue at or for each cottage, but in the geometry of it, they were as if they belonged, because each statue was a double figure, fixed, although when I drew closer I saw they were moving, and what I thought was wrestling seemed more as a dance of sorts, but awkward, as dancers perhaps affectionately wrestling, eerie in the sunshine, and the long beautiful grass in the valley.

I saw that one of each double figure was a white man, and that the other of him was a monster or a creature, and though of a different coloring, extraordinary as afar of color, darker than the other, but the same height, yet heavier, and extremely powerful. Each monster had different features, more different than each white man was different from the other white men, although the white men seemed to be keepers, which perhaps accounted for their friendly and sophisticated group expression.

They all apparently knew what they were doing, and in a friendly and courteous way, they cautioned me.

The monster, or animal, closest to me was much like a dolphin, and with all that creature's power, standing on its tail and facing its keeper it yet turned, as the keeper cautioned me, and it almost—perhaps it did—it smiled, and I heard a sonic laugh of delight. The keeper laughed too, and said I shouldn't come much closer. I was a few feet away, but I suddenly liked, although feared, the creature, that I wanted to be closer to it. I didn't move, though, and in that sense, I looked around the valley.

The keepers and creatures were all struggling, or dancing, or wrestling, all on their feet. One creature had horny fins on its back, a huge grinning jaw, huge hind legs and little dangling front legs the fingers of which were or seemed almost like puppy-dog's paws, and there were no chains, ropes, or wires, each was free and moving, and each keeper held each creature not by the forelegs or paws, or throat, but as by or along the shoulders, and as I went, I waved and smiled goodbye, and they did likewise, still dancing, or wrestling. Keeper and creature, although it wasn't as if I had been there that I was leaving something behind which I couldn't understand, it was tearing in me, and treasured, as something ancient, vast and unknown, yet familiar, clear, and simple.

An Encounter

The Boy in the Body of a Man

1

I hadn't seen Blaze since he'd gone out to California on a three week lecture tour, and it was by coincidence that we ran into each other on the street near where I live. A happy coincidence! and after we had embraced and exchanged greetings and outcries, we went to our neighborhood bar which is very pleasant in the afternoon, still, for a few cool ones. It was a couple of minutes after two.

I asked him how the trip had been and as he seemed tired and yet a little angry, I used a certain tone of voice in my question which I knew he liked. It had, he said, been wonderful, but was playing hell with his work, and he feared he wouldn't be able to write a poem for several weeks, until he recovered from meeting so many young people, and from reading so many manuscripts. 'I hear their voices,' he said, and put his face in his hands and his elbows on the bar. He rubbed his face, lowered his hands, looked at me and shook his head saying he was absolutely *sick* of poetry.

His sipped his drink, wiped his lips with the soft small square paper napkin, and frowning, asked me if I had a little while to spare? I replied that I did. He had met, he said, and had an argument with a young man who reminded him of something which had happened several years ago, and he had thought of me to tell it to because I was a prose writer and this he said was a prose narrative. He also said that he was alarmed because he was turning fifty, and his interest in young women and girls and on occasion boys, was getting out of hand, and he had realized in California that what it was was a yearn for contact with his youth, which frightened him.

He sipped his drink, and with a frown, stared into space. Then he asked me if I ever felt that the things that went on in the outside world were reflections of what went on within us, and I said yes. Blaze nodded, and again sipping his drink, turned and looked at me with an intent gaze. He sighed.

In the tone, he said, of the beginning of The Turn of the Screw he had had an extraordinary experience a few years ago, the meaning of which he had found out last week in Los Angeles.

I looked at him. Blaze. Thoughtful, angry and worried.

Guy Blaze was and still is a part of me. A very real part. A man about five feet ten with a paunch and thin legs, big hands, smallish shoulders and a big head. His eyes are grey-blue, his hair is light brown and fixed in close curls atop his head. His nose is aquiline and his lips are thin, but cherry-red. The French cigarettes he (as I) smoke, have slightly discolored his teeth and fingertips. It seems incredible that we have known each other so long.

We went to the same high school together. A small school in a small town in Ohio. Clyde, in fact.

He had been a famous poet then, and later went on to greater fame, while I struggled to become a novelist and became instead an essayist, with a reputation based on, unhappily, book reviews.

I was forty-five years old and years and years before had been in 8th grade when he had graduated, and though I lost touch with him I managed to keep track of him through the editor of the town newspaper, and Guy's folks. After I had graduated, I went to Ohio State for two years, was drafted, and served (twenty two months and three weeks two days). Blaze had claimed Conscientious Objector status and won it, and spent his two years doing road and farm work. I had been overseas when I had been in the service, and a couple of years after I'd gotten out, I returned to Europe, and one afternoon, walking along the Left Bank, and admiring Notre Dame, I stopped in a cafe, had a couple of Ricards, looked at the river and the great Cathedral before me, rose from my table and covering my bill and leaving a tip, I turned down a side street, and having taken a brief walk, I saw a small bookstore called The American Bookstore, and I ambled over, glanced at the books on display, and there in the window saw a very handsome hard cover edition of *The Messenger*, a book of poems by Guy Blaze, so I hastily went into the bookstore, and to my left I saw Blaze himself, standing in a patch of sunlight, reading his own book.

I went to him. He looked up, grinned, and admitted it wasn't a bad book at all, and that he thought he was a pretty good poet.

You always were, I said.

We shook hands on that happy note, I mean he was happy (I was amused), and as it gradually began to dawn on him who I was, he gradually began to wake up, so we returned to the café where I'd just been, and as I was able to answer many of the questions he had about childhood friends, and the girls, too, we had a marvelous afternoon, and to make a long story short, we've been friends together ever since.

Later, back in the States, we used to use each other's names, we were incredibly alike, and we imitated each other's styles, in talking as well as in writing, and most especially in reviewing books: a job that I had anyway, and one that he got just to continue our fun. He reviewed books of stories, novels, essays, etc., and I reviewed poetry, each of us working for the two competing evening newspapers in town, the editors never knew the difference except once, which was by chance, and most amusing. In the same (evening) edition of each paper, by chance I had compared a book of poems to Blaze's (while praising him), and he had done likewise with a novel (praising me), which caused a lot of laughter between the two of us, and our friends, and otherwise some rather curious gossip, which led, inevitably, to our dismissal. There were a lot of writers and poets who were angry, thinking it was a plot: we were out to get a monopoly on the local literary scene.

In the years that followed, when we were together— he travelled a lot—and when delightfully drunk we called each other by the other's name, and to the pleasure of everyone, spoke aloud what the other would say, so it was in the sense of knowing him very well, and he me, that we could be each other. He was and is a mellow and marvelous man, independent of any single dictatorial emotion except romance, so that afternoon when we were together in the bar, the day after (it turned out) that he'd returned from California, when he said the following, I was impressed, and reasonably so.

"This business of turning fifty," he said soberly, "is no joke, and I am more than slightly obsessed with those BEAUTIFUL young women, and the girls—you know? I'll tell you, my friend, I feel like an adult teenager! *obsessed* with youth!"

I nodded. It was happening to me, too, though I was almost five years his junior, but as he appeared to have a story in mind, and as I was a more than willing listener— he was a great story-teller—I relaxed in the comfortable chair at the bar, and as each of us had a fresh cool drink before us, I relaxed, and listened to his story.

2

Despair, he said, sadly, depression, violence and terror come to me in their worldly combinations, and mixed with my own guilt because I am so habit-formed in my ways, I have a sense of myself as failure, and the failure is complete. My awareness of my self as habit-formed equals my awareness of the world in trouble: that troubled outer world.

The knowledge that my life is a sort of figure-skater dancing through the varieties of formed habits is as depressing as anything I know, and it shows up in the most simple ways. I go places, I am at places, in places, to places, park benches, parties, movie theatres, beaches, and I don't want to be there, and yet I stay! But while I'm staying I know I should leave! But—therefore I get angry at myself, and extremely short tempered, dissatisfied, and just plain grumpy, and I tend to take it out on others. I project. And occasionally it has been dangerous.

"Unconsciously," I said.

"Yes," Blaze said, "but just barely. Almost conscious, but not quite."

Semi-conscious, I thought, and said so—that's it! he cried, it's when I'm semi-conscious.

It isn't nearly as bad as it was, he said, apologetically, and I agreed. He had worked hard. Cranky, grumpy, moody were synonyms for semi-consciousness, and as the impact of each is so kin to limbo it was like an ethereal hell, insubstantial so that the first-person I can't get hold of it.

Forgive the lecture, he said. But I'm working on myself which is why it's important I do what I want, and why I'm angry and depressed about the lecture tour, because it took me away from poems I wanted to write.

Blaze's writing consciousness, like my own, isn't transient: neither of us can write on the road. What we do therefore, we experience that road.

3

Did I ever tell you that I once met a Mafia hit-man? Blaze asked me. Yes, and I shook hands with him. I couldn't see a thing in his eyes and I didn't know what to do with my hand after I'd used it to take his hand—but this was years ago when I was in my twenties, and as you prose writers would say, years pass and the scene changes: a new narrative begins: cinematic calendar pages fly by and there's a friendly fellow I came to know not very well who was a bore after Hello, how are you, and after a bottle of Bud, the ball scores and sixty seconds of shop talk, any dialogue was hopeless, although (he, and) I actually tried. Yes. I was pleased to see him at the bar, hoping he would perhaps change and become interesting, but I was wrong again. He was the kind of guy who can be around in the sense of a story everybody knows, like the Rigby woman, and we were, after all, there in the barroom together.

In retrospect, I am being unfair, because he was pleasant to watch ballgames with, and for me to say he was a bore is to admit that once again I expected him to be something which he wasn't and couldn't be—see, that semi-consciousness again. I took out my own irritation at myself on him. Well, however that may have been, I mean as wrong as I was, it was how the whole thing happened. I was in a semi-conscious limbo that night. I had a lot of money then, and as I lived alone (this was before I met Dotty), there were nights when I didn't know what to do with myself. A situation, as we well know, that can make for curious happenings.

I think it was his voice. He couldn't help it. He had a voice which Budweiser lubricated, and the words came from his throat and nose at once, like a nasal ooga in such loudness that made my eardrums tremble, and in the most routine dialogue I often placed my hand on his arm and smiled, saying Hey pal, keep it down a little? whereupon he lowered his voice and smiled himself, until the next slug of Bud, although he seemed a little confused. He wasn't deaf, either, although he had that loud way of talking.

That night he had been invited to a party by a bunch of guys and gals at the office. It was in somebody's apartment on St. Charles Place, and he asked me if I wanted (Blaze sighed) to go along. I had been drinking that evening towards perhaps another self that would know what to do with me, but I hadn't yet made contact, I was still a little separated and I couldn't make up my mind what to do when he asked and kept saying aw c'mon it'll be fun, there'll be lots of booze, and I most certainly did not want to go, which is why I said Yes, to not, as the story goes, outfox myself, but to be able to get away from the attempt to reach a self, and that, my Lucky love, is how the whole mess happened. I *puzzled* him! Which goes to show what an asshole a forty-four year old poet can be (I was forty-four then), when he's semi-conscious and

Separated, I said.

Right, he said, and took a gulp from his drink, looked at me, and wagging his index finger at me, said,

True, *but* I had wanted to say *something* about those near-android killers Kennedy sent over, with their little green tams. Remember?

I nodded: did I *ever!*

Okay, Blaze said, I didn't know where I was, but suddenly, or maybe gradually, I was sitting on a long sofa beside an end table to my left, which had a lamp on it. I was smoking a cigarette and not looking at any of the business guys and their dates who were enjoying themselves jammed and twisting together in the apartment, a St. Charles Place apartment near where the man who lived with Lillian Hellman had died, and this metropolitan apartment was standard: kitchen to the left as you came in, living room stretched out before you, and at the end of the left was the bedroom, and the bathroom. The curtains were open at the far end of the living room opposite the front door, and there was a down-Metropolis view. From the twenty-sixth floor.

The guys were wearing summer suits and their girls were in summer dresses, they danced to the Beatles, Donovan, the early Stones, etc., the ashtrays were filled with dead Kents, and as my pal with the ooga voice which Budweiser uncorked, had vanished, I sat alone, angry at myself for being where I was (where was I?), and for not being down-Met where I even then wasn't sure I wanted to be. I had a drink in my hand, I noticed, and it was cold, which meant many things, all obvious, so I took a sip which revived me a little, and with the wall of bodies dancing before me to music which hung on a thunderblast—I stared into space. Nobody knew me. It formed a sort of stupor. I was at somebody's party, somewhere. I was a famous poet and I was drunk and alone, and before I burst into tears I thought I would take a sip, a little nip, which I did, which refreshed me, and just as I thought I would put my drink on the end table, and fold my hands in my lap, lean back and take a little nap, a small voice, like Stevenson's Bottle Imp, cried:

"Look!"

My eyes popped open!

At arm's length before me—no further, there wasn't room—I saw a young man, in fact a boyish looking youth, tall, lean, handsome and cool, who faced and was talking with, a young woman sitting opposite him. Each was seated on a chair. He was relaxed, and she was upset.

What did she look like, I asked.

Guy Blaze looked at me patiently. Lucky? he asked, don't you know?

I did, I smiled, but I wanted to hear him tell me.

She was an attractive young white Christian with sensitive but naive eyes who made $9,000 a year, shared an apartment on Ivy with two other women, and they all wore blue summer dresses and hadn't yet switched to silver necklaces and bracelets because their mothers wore gold.

She'd lined her eyes lightly, put stuff on her eyelashes, had rouge on her cheeks, and pale red on her lips and I was insane therefore I knew. She wore a slip and a bra, her hair was sprayed, she wore low high heels and was self-conscious in a not-so-unconscious prayer that guys see her through it all, and as she made brief frustrated gestures with her hands I saw her nails were painted, and I realized she was angry and couldn't find the words to express it. Miss America was in trouble: her eyes were drawn down, her eyebrows were up, and she gestured and finally, helplessly, pleaded:

How could you?

Well ma'am, he smiled, you see it was my job.

But—she cried—searching for the words, and with an intensity that sharpened my vision and brought me wide awake: she leaned forward, towards him, and said, gesturing—she was very near tears—to him:

That's—that's *wrong!*

He nodded, and smiled again. I know, he said rather tonelessly, war's wrong. But when you're in it—he gestured sympathetically—you do like they say: you follow orders.

He looked at her. She looked at him and scowled.

She clenched her fists and bit her lip, emotionally and intellectually unable to find the words, and while she was fighting to find them, I had a chance to look at him closely, and to figure out or think clearly about, his face, which was handsome enough, and youthful because it had no lines. His face was boyish, in fact, and tan, like his hands, and like the sides of his long, artistic, but powerful fingers, his skull was narrow along the temples, and he had a high forehead under a soft ash-blonde crewcut. His eyebrows were ash-blonde too. His eyes were grey and blue and extremely clear with tiny, almost floating, nail-head pupils, and his nose just missed being turned up. His lips were thin and humorless. He had a strong jaw. He wore a yellow sport shirt and light grey slacks. He was extremely powerful in his arms, wrists and hands. Yet he looked innocent, and rather confused, there, with all those people. He looked like a boy in the body of a man. And there I was, looking at him. I was a fool to have gone there. I was twice his age, and I was wearing an orange sweatshirt, worn bluejeans and worn sneakers. No socks. I sipped my drink. A hippie. Cary Grant.

He adopted the pose of a relaxed farmer: legs stretched out and ankles crossed, and shoulders slightly curved forward as he sat back in the chair, with his hands on the arms of the chair, except when he leaned forward towards her, to explain something. But his ankles stayed crossed, and only his hands moved, and they not very much.

I had heard her telling him he had a nice tan and then I had heard him saying thanks, just back from overseas. Then I had heard, which was when I had decided to take a nap, her asking him where he had been and when he said Vietnam my eyes snapped open, and when she asked him what he had done in Vietnam, because he looked like a boyish kind of engineer, and he had said he was in Special Forces, and some of the color ran out of her face, as she asked, and as I sat up and lit a cigarette: Were you a Green Beret?

He smiled and said, Yes ma'am, and my blood ran cold.

I had a perfect view of their profiles, and each of them sat before me, not two feet away. The lamp to my left, on the end table, was not tall enough to light my face, so they weren't aware of me. But I saw their faces perfectly. Two white faces, in profile, as she asked,

"Did you kill people?"

He nodded, with his face adjusted to explain.

His gaze was like two straight lines, briefed, remembering his orders. She said, as her face gathered in anxiety and grief—not a pleasant sight—

"I know this goes on in war," she said, "but this is such an *awful* war, so many women and children have died, and how, I mean *why*, you're a good-looking guy! *how* could you—you—*be—in*—that—"

We had to, he said, simply.

31

But why? I mean in that *way*, although I know, but the *way*—

We were trained for it, he explained.

She put the knuckles of her right hand against her lips. Her face suddenly wrenched, as her eyes widened in a combination of pain and anger toward the look of a hard stare, as she shook her head and murmured that wasn't it at all. She shook her head briefly, but forcefully.

Don't you! she cried, don't you know this whole thing is WRONG?

Soberly, he looked at her. "We're doing the best we can," he quoted.

She wrung her hands in frustration with his literalness. I leaned forward and said Excuse me:

"I know you."

He smiled, pretty close to a grin, but he was puzzled and he searched my face. His eyes were direct.

Where did we meet? he asked, silently.

We haven't met, I said.

When, he smiled, because he knew who I was too, he asked, Then how do you know me?

Because of your eyes, I said.

His gaze hardened a little, like diamonds getting cold, and he said, while the young woman looked at me in alarm, he asked,

What about my eyes?

I lit a cigarette and said aw come on, and he grinned, and said no, no kidding, what about my eyes? and I said, you know about them, and he said, excitedly, or in a rush, no, no I don't, tell me, I'd like to know!

I gestured to her: What do you think she's been talking about?

He blinked, and looked at me. I puffed smoke, and he changed tactic, and with his psychology, and as drunk as I was I had that old feeling I was once again flirting with a direct form of self-destruction through a masochistic combination of flirtation and anger, as he asked me, a little of his violence rising, he was being careful, and he was calm and smiling:

Who are you? You don't know me!

I nodded, and he wasn't sure what I was nodding to, so I let him figure it out and he did. He asked me why I thought I knew him, when I didn't, and I said it was because of his eyes, and he said—asked, rather, what it was about his eyes that made me know him, and I said that it was murder.

"Murder?" he asked. He made a coy smile. He made a Saturday Evening Post whistle.

More than a little frightened, and wondering what I thought I was, I puffed my cigarette, and again nodded. I said: "That's why she's afraid of you, and upset by you." I gestured to her.

She was frightened, and of me too.

He frowned because he thought she was against the war, not him, which was true, and what she couldn't understand: how he could have done those things, sitting there before her. And I admit that I wanted to say to him those things she couldn't, and as I was feeling pretty strange about saying anything, I yet wanted to say something directly, and in that sense I used her. To get to him. He had been briefed on her, but not on me.

She was about to deny—to say that wasn't what she meant, when I gave her a hard look, which made her angry, but she bit her lip and stayed put in her position in this little conflict, and suddenly I felt bad in my manipulation of her, so I said to him look: "It's what I see in your eyes, not hers. I apologize—" and I extended my hands in a brief gesture, to her, and said that I really was sorry, but then, I realized she didn't know what I was talking about or apologizing for, and they both looked at me. I felt a little wave of drunkenness arise, so I repeated what I'd said before, that I saw murder. I saw it, not her, because what she saw—or better yet, couldn't see, was him volunteering to commit the murder.

He carefully lit a filtertip with his Zippo, and after blowing smoke to one side, looked at me. He was as clean as his fingernails, which were spotless. There was, I knew, nothing about him that smelled.

We looked at each other, and I made a decision. Blaze grinned: In the spirit in the understanding that truth is a stranger to (not stranger than) fiction, I said, and I did:

"You like it."

Well he didn't like that. He asked me like what, and I said killing.

The young woman made a little noise, rose from the chair and departed into the wall of dancing bodies. He watched her leave and then swerved his hard grey-blue gaze on me. I had gone too far: I'd made the killer uncomfortable scaring the wits out of me, because his eyes, which were on me were sending me a message, *How do you know? You're not one of us.*

He leaned toward me a little, face slightly averted and eyes sliding in slits, ear out like in the jungle. He wanted to know and he looked at me, and made a thin white smile. From some distant place that made my anger rise, and after finishing my glass of courage, which refreshed me, I said, bravely,

I'm not afraid of you, as terrified as I am of you, because I know you.

He shook his head and took my stiff-upper-lip literally: "You don't know me," he said, but his eyes never left mine, and I was witnessing his carefully trained unconscious rising, "and," he added, which sent a chill down my spine: "I don't know you."

I nodded, because he was telling me to lay off. So,

34

having gotten the message, and rather glad he had ended it (I thought), I decided to obey orders.

I rose from the sofa, and saying I was going into the kitchen for a drink, I left him sitting there. My standing body pushed into the mob of dancers. But I looked back. He was looking at his hands. The back of his head, at the neck, was impossibly vulnerable, and I felt guilty. I turned, and headed through the crowd, to the kitchen.

I entered the kitchen. There were many bottles and lemons, limes, and mixers on the counter in the typically small area. I made myself a drink, sipped it, it tasted good, and I leaned against the sink and stared at the floor and thought about what I had just realized, even then realizing something more dangerous than I knew. I decided I'd find the Budweiser ooga-voice, tell him so long, and catch a cab down-Met to the bar, this bar—

I nodded.

Which I eventually did. I caught a cab on Horizon, but in the growing realization that if I didn't get out of there fast, something larger than I could handle was going to happen, I realized I was in fact just plain drunk, so I took a sip of my drink to straighten myself out, which it did, and while I was going through these changes the boy in the body of a man came into the kitchen and walked directly to me. He stood before me and smiled. His blue eyes were unmoving, like him watching Mom when she looked in the mirror.

The kitchen was narrow instead of squarish, and the far end, where I was, by the sink, wasn't nine feet across, and as I was leaning against the sink, which was in the center, so other people at the party could come in and I wouldn't be in their way, there wasn't much room on either side of me, and in fact I could stretch out my arms and touch cabinets on either side. He took a step or two and stood exactly in front of me, and without smiling, said, honestly:

"Tell me that stuff about my eyes again."

So. Like a boy with a toy, an object or an alien organism he could control but not understand, he looked at me. But his eyes didn't change, and as I was at a curious loss for words because I hadn't thought of him recently, I began to panic, but seeing the emergency, I came to my rescue.

You've been trained to kill. You enjoy it.

He came so close to me we almost touched. He put his hands over my shoulders onto the cabinets behind me, but just above my shoulders, and not an inch away from my ears, so that we were face to face between his arms, and tilting his head to one side his eyes focused on mine. It was the way guys used to move in for the kill, get her in the kitchen and kiss her. He moved in, and with his lips nearly touching mine, and his eyes hard and steady, he parted his lips and said, tenderly, *Tell me.*

His teeth were white, perfect, and brutal, and yet, somehow, face to face with this brainwashed hired killer, and though I was terrified, I was also angry, because I knew him, and in a single crystallized consciousness of guns, napalm, helicopters, genocide and little peasants in thatch huts, I clenched my teeth as he whispered his question again: "Tell me—" oh tell me, tell me, I spoke into the warm breath from his mouth, *I see murder.*

He breathed softly, How can you? How? he whispered, almost pleading, with his boy's breath, and his deadly hands so close to me, "What—tell me, again, tell me how!" he implored, yet in the subtle greed in a boy's wish.

I let him have it in three little words.

I see nothing.

He drew back with his eyes widening in a reaction I couldn't understand, a sort of whirl, and with an invisible clap of his hands, he pointed at my chest, and said, his blue eyes wide and almost white with excitement:

"Wait here! I'll be right back! I'm gonna get my buddy!"

He quickly left the kitchen.

I stood in shock. Frozen, absolutely, in that spot: *buddy*, I thought, *buddy*? So there are *two* of them?

I spun off into a kind of orbit, but was also suspended, and in the memory of what the Turks did to T. E. Lawrence, I finished the drink in a gulp, and was as sober as a brain surgeon.

I placed the glass on the counter, rapidly left the kitchen, made my way through the dancers, opened the front door and stepped out into the corridor where I stopped.

The elevator was exactly across the hall.

I took three steps, and pushed the button. The indicating light didn't go on. The panel was black. I pushed the button again. Nothing. And with all my voices, including the voice of that blasted imp, calling me all the hateful things and names they could think of, I raced down the corridor to my left, went around the corner to find the exit stairs, they weren't there, so I ran back the way I had come, and tried the other end, pushing the elevator button as I passed. Nothing happened. There was nothing to be found down the other corridor, either, except rows of anonymous doors.

I went back to the elevator and willed it to rise. I pushed the button. Nothing. I stood there, perspiring and trembling. I felt, in the sight and the sound, that double-headed creature from out of the jungle come bounding out into the corridor for some fun, and torture, and the light blinked on. It worked its way, blinking up from the first floor, slowly, as I stood with my hands clenched against my temples. It flashed 26, the doors opened, I leaped inside and pushed 1, and the doors stayed open. I pushed the CLOSE button, then again and then again, nothing happened, as I stood there, wildly staring at that apartment door exactly across from me, as I heard the laughter and music, and the elevator door slowly slid shut, and it began its slow descent.

It stopped at its appointed mechanical place, Lobby, which was 1, and when the doors slid open I ran out, went down three steps and across the marble floor, and like The Invisible Man I fluttered the astonished doorman, as I opened the two sets of glass doors instead of going through them.

I found myself on a cross-Metropolis street, and not knowing where I was except that I was on St. Charles Place, I ran vast discovering Horizon Avenue, which was one-way, down-Met traffic only, I ran into, and up the Avenue towards the rapidly moving machines seeing that pair of empty eyes before me I saw a bright yellow light, a vacant cab, and approaching fast. I ran to it, yelled in through the driver's open window: "Down-Met!" and as the cab slowed—not much, either—as brakes hit and tires shrieked, I opened the rear door, dove in and closed the door behind me and collapsed on the seat.

"Down-Met," I croaked. Yeah, the cabbie said, down-Met where?

I told her.

She nodded, and after she adjusted the meter, we sped along. I sat back, lit a cigarette, and thought about what had happened, and slowly came to my senses, thus deciding that no matter how angry I was at myself, I'd never —ever—again play with a killer's unconscious in flirtation with the boy I used to be.

I nodded. We finished our drinks, and ordered two more. Blaze asked me what I thought.

You're growing up, I responded.

If I don't I'll kill myself on the way, he said. Then he smiled: Or he will. He paused, and said, as much to himself as to me, Does it ever stop? and turning to me, as I nodded no, except to those in complete control, he asked, Do you think I'll make it?

Why not? I grinned. You're almost fifty.

Another Encounter

Lucky Star

I walked briskly along the street among summer afternoon traffic, and when I came to the corner of Thirve I stopped. Just beyond the traffic light, near a public telephone booth, I saw an older woman lying face up in the street, one arm out, dress up to her thighs, and her purse on the asphalt near a bag with a few groceries that had spilled from it, and as I reached her side taking off my sports jacket as I did so, the human ghouls began to drift in, and stood and stared down at her.

She was near enough to the curb to not be in any danger from passing machines, and I folded up my jacket, knelt in the street beside her, lifted her head and put my jacket underneath. Her hair was thin, and grey. I smiled down to her frightened brown eyes, lowered her dress carefully, and said she need not worry, help is on the way.

She was, obviously, in shock. Her eyes, though glassy, seemed to register what I had said, and she appeared to watch my face as I took her pulse, which was below normal but not dangerously so. About ten ghouls had gathered around, with more coming. I had been on the scene about sixty seconds. I looked up, and searching the group, I found a man, a white man in a seersucker suit. I said:

"Phone the cops."

He was astonished! I said, "And tell them to bring an ambulance."

Having been startled into consciousness, he turned on his heel and walked toward and into the phone booth. I saw him dial the number and glance at me while he did so. I turned again to the woman, took out my handkerchief and wiped her brow. She was around sixty, Jewish, and terrified. Her lips were moving, and again I reassured her that help was coming. So were the ghouls, of various races and creeds, and they watched me gather the woman's groceries, and purse, and put them safely at her side. I gently touched her skull behind her ears, and thought I felt a lump behind her left.

The man I had told to telephone the cops joined me, and with a bright look in his eyes—delighted to be conscious—he said they were on their way—with an ambulance, and I thanked him. The ghouls stared.

A novelty.

I took her left hand in both of mine, and as I gazed briefly into her eyes, which were silently asking me what had happened, I heard a siren. Getting closer, as I held her hand. Again, in the big bad city, help was coming quickly. In two or three minutes it was over.

The ambulance was parked on an angle, the attendants had lifted her onto a stretcher and slid her into the rear of the machine. I'd given them my estimate of her pulse, I didn't wear a watch, and told them to check the back of her head and her heart. I felt a little self-conscious because they were slightly ghoulish themselves, and among the ghouls that had gathered, had they taken over? But the two young cops who arrived gave out some looks that had the ghouls been conscious, would have humiliated them. One of the cops was taking notes—doing paperwork—in his book, and the other asked me what happened and I told him. I thought she had fallen backwards off the curb. Anything I can do? I asked.

He shook his head. No, he said. Lucky you showed up, he added.

Lucky for her, I gestured, to the ambulance which was driving away, but when I looked at him, his eyes were hard, and he shook his head, No, he said, lucky for you.

I looked away, nearly blushing. Yeah, I murmured, you're right, and since it was in the afternoon and the sun was on its way down, there was a sort of glow around the cop's hat, and I saw then, an emanation of long thin rods of gold that formed a circle near his temples as I stammered Thanks for coming so fast. She was in shock, but still very frightened.

He didn't nod or say anything and feeling like I was talking too much, as I always feel in these things, this was his job, after all, vision from the bottom up, I was embarrassed, and humble, standing beside him. Smoothly, but very suddenly, he moved to the collection of ghouls and said as to helpless animals, Okay, it's over, beat it. Go on, beat it.

They began to disperse. I made a so-long gesture to the cop who nodded, our eyes met briefly, and in my embarrassment I made my way out through the thinning crowd, crossed on the green light, did the shopping for supper and headed home.

When I told Blaze about it the next evening at supper, he admitted he was jealous, and I asked why.

Well, he said, because you are lucky.

Feeling self-conscious and embarrassed all over again, I said it was true, in a spiritual sense, but—

The cop saw it, Blaze said.

Saw what? I asked, feeling dense. The adjective? I laughed.

The noun, Blaze chuckled. No, you're Lucky, because of your transference to the cop. In this instance, positive, which he realized, and reasonably, in his consideration, thought you were lucky to do it, and in a more conversational sense would with plain speech call you Lucky.

"Lucky, darling," my wife Audrey said, "would you bring the other bottle of wine in?"

I rose, and went into the kitchen, and as I opened the refrigerator door I heard Audrey say to Blaze's wife Dotty: He is Lucky. Guy, you're right.

Love is a verb, Blaze said, irrationally, and as I emerged from the kitchen with the wine, I heard Blaze, and saw him too, as he sighed, pursed his lips, and with a rather winsome gaze to the ceiling, he said, Lucky, softly, a star is born.

Blaze's Request

Both our wives work. Audrey is a copy reader at Forum, and Dotty is an assistant editor at Victor. Thus Blaze and I have the weekdays to ourselves, which is why when he misses a day, he is so upset, because he realizes how fortunate he is—so do I, but I can miss a day or so, and not get as upset as Blaze. Anyway, both of us get up early, and while Blaze and Dotty have breakfast, so do myself and Audrey, and after the women go to work, Blaze and I go to our respective typewriters.

We work until about three in the afternoon. Then we wash the dishes, make the beds, clean our places up, and do the shopping and, if necessary, the laundry. Then we meet at the bar.

On a snowy afternoon late last year, or perhaps early this year, Blaze and I had met as usual, each of us with our bags of groceries, and he asked me to write a novel of the stories we'd told each other.

He was more mellow and eloquent than usual because he had gotten there before me, and hadn't, I could tell, had the two unusually solid meals I'd had. He was glowing too soon. I was very hungry that day, and I didn't know why, but I was and I had three eggs, bacon and *grits* (which I love), for breakfast, and a hunk of cheddar cheese, some tomato slices and a half pound of liver for lunch, which is why around three thirty the vodka tasted so delicious.

I placed my groceries on the bar first, though, and pulled up a barstool next to Blaze, sat down, rubbed my hands together exclaiming upon the cold outdoors, and watched while the bartender, Frank, made my drink. Blaze put his hand on my shoulder, and I glanced at him. Without much or in fact no preface at all, he said rather thoughtfully, that he wished he could write prose. Then, he looked at me. Aw Lucky, he said, in response to the face I made.

"You're so full of beans you oughta be canned," I said.

Blaze held up his hand and intoned Peace, my friend. Peace. What I mean is I wish I could write prose like *you*.

That's different, I admitted.

Yes, he said, it is. And I've been thinking about it. To really do it. Write a book, a novel even, in that way you have, of these afternoons we've spent together.

You mean, I said, that you want me to write your book.

"Yes," he said, and chuckled.

How about if I write *my* book?

Write *our* book, he smiled.

My face brightened: okay, "I will!" I cried. Let's have another! Frank! We downed our drinks.

We caught his attention, a great bartender. Great. He took our glasses, rock glasses, they were, added ice, a twist of lemon, and filled 'em to the brim with Popov Vodka.

Frank, I said, did you know that the word *vodka*, in Russian, means little water?

Frank laughed. Blaze said, Where did you get that?

Yesterday's paper, I said, and paid Frank, with a ten.

That's pretty good, Frank said. Little water. He rang it up and gave me change. I passed him a dollar and asked him to put it in his butterfly collection. He had a way of folding dollar bills so they looked like butterflies, or bow ties, before he put them in his tip cup.

Frank took it, folded it in that way, and dropped it in the cup, turned, leaned across the bar, looked me square in the eyes, smiled, slapped me on the shoulder, and said You're *all right* Lucky, my friend!

We laughed.

You too, Guy, Frank said enthusiastically: you're terrific! Both of you!

Two businessmen came in, shook the snow off their coats and sat at the other end of the bar, and as Frank walked towards them they greeted him, and after shaking hands with them, they gave their orders, and we watched him make two dry Metropolises.

Frank had given a little party last fall, and had invited us. Bring the wives, too, Frank had said. It had been a really pleasant friendly Sunday.

The snow light from the front window made the glasses sparkle on the bar, and in the sparkle I felt the mystery of the afternoon.

We lit up, and puffed from our cigarettes. Blaze said, with thought:

47

But Lucky, what will be the title?

The name of the title story, I offered.

Good, he said, yes, you've done that in the past, so we won't know until you write that story. Good. Maybe you could begin here! I trust your judgement.

I laughed: "Yeah?"

He affected a hurt expression, and, in a little voice, said, well I do.

Then he leaned forward: Pound said, I think, Blaze said, that greatness in a work of art means it is continually fresh. So make your book great in its freshness. I see in you Lucky, a speech as plain as the ground, and that's what we need.

You do, eh, I said. You see that.

I do, he said. Make it warm, he continued, as he looked over my shoulder to the front window, and beyond. He stared into space. He sipped vodka.

"Make it warm, fertile, talkative, and in the event of reading, imaginative. Reveal its mutations in an organic narrative that will read like the discovery of a new dawn!"

A new drink? I asked. Russian vodka from a freezing pewter mug—

A *Grand Illusion!* he cried, in French.

Sure thing, I said.

He sipped his drink, and fell silent, his eyes searching my face.

What I like most about you Blaze, I commented, is your attitude, the continuity of your attitude found in the pronouncing of your last name, having added an accent over the e in it, so that it rhymes with a as in hay, get it?

Clever, he said, and leaned towards me, tapped me on the knee, and added: but not necessarily original.

He sat back. He smiled like a cat, then made a sudden little gasp.

You're just jealous, I laughed.

He sighed, looked at his drink, raised it, and sipped, and lowering it, looked at me. That could be, he admitted. That could very well be.

I sipped my drink, puffed from my cigarette, and tapped an ash in the ashtray on the bar.

Will you write it? he asked.

Of course, I said. Didn't I say I would?

Blaze sang: Penny Lane is in my ears and in my eyes da da da dee dum, —

Penny Lane!

She's Going Home

Into the Future

I showed the following manuscript to Blaze, famous poet though he was (and you should forgive me that, in light of what is to come), asking him what he thought of it. He saw that it was brief, brevity is a concern of his, and after I'd made him a cup of coffee, he agreed to read it. His Majesty slowly took his reading glasses out of his jacket pocket—the round ones, with steel rims—put them on, and sitting in Audrey's rocking chair by the front windows, read it. 'Fantastic,' he muttered, and read on. 'Chilling,' he added, and as I washed the dishes, made the bed, and went over the floor with a dust mop, Blaze finished it, looked at me and asked me where I'd gotten

Finue from. We both laughed. I didn't answer him.

"Yes," he said. The too single voice is your worry, but in this one it's necessary. This is single narrative: two witnessed by one. Blaze gave me the manuscript and said Good, it's the only chance to the future.

Late in a late October twilight on the bottom of the vertical metropolis, the microcosmic first person (me), crossed red Illinois and headed vast towards Finue. The street on which I walked was deserted except for a small woman who was slightly hunched over, and walking— cowering actually, along close to the marble fronted concrete walls on the inside side of the sidewalk. I walked on the outside near the gutter so my tall figure would not alarm her, but I realized she was alarmed anyway, so I said, as I was just about to pass her, Don't be afraid, I'm just walking by. She turned, and her face was pale, but in the twilight, even more pale. But. She thanked me, and we both stopped and looked at each other.

"I'm so frightened these days," she said, and her voice trembled: "I'm afraid of everything."

I nodded, and expressed my sorrow, knowing indeed that to have that fear in the metropolis is horrible, and makes anxiety an ocean of torment, and apprehension a terror of every move. She said,

I'm so alone.

"Where do you live?" I asked.

She pointed towards Finue and said just up ahead there, in an apartment house. I said,

Well look, I'm walking this way anyway, may I walk you home?

She smiled, and we began walking slowly, vast. In the gloom.

"My husband just died," she said, "and I don't know what to do without him," we've been together so many years.

I nodded, and murmured that I was sorry.

A machine drifted by. I asked her if she had any friends.

She shook her head. No. No one except the neighbors in the apartment house into which she and her husband had moved last year, so when a few months later her husband had died, it meant, though she didn't say it, her friends were people she didn't know, and who didn't know her, but lived on the same floor, and from the tone in her voice they were the people who say good morning and good evening as they leave from, and return to, their own apartments, citizens, each afraid themselves: four-limbed human nuclei in concrete cells with a complicated system of wires and electricity for communication.

"My children are grown and married with children of their own, and all live away from here," she said, meaning she didn't want to bother them, and in the tone under her trembling voice I heard a decision slowly being made, and, in the form of a deep breath I felt it was more common sense, than intuitive, but an extraforce common sense, which to younger people seems dazzling, and brilliant, and wise to the Nth degree, true enough in impact, but plain speech to the older people who speak the words. She was gradually approaching a realization, and she was her only means to it. It was only through her and it would emerge from her as she was, because the realization was as she was and would become, so she would rather be alone in her fear, than alarm others with it.

We crossed Finue which is not busy or brightly lighted or happily noisy in twilight, not in that neighborhood, and she pointed to the white brick apartment house across the street, so we crossed over. It looked pleasant. Casement windows and ivy, with a flower box here and there.

I kept the slow pace with her, and when we reached the front door, which was three steps down, I went first and held the outer door open for her:

You'll be okay—

"Yes," she said, "Thankyou."

The man in the blue uniform in the lobby smiled to her as she went inside. I had held the inner security door open, too, after he had buzzed her in. He gave me a sharp look, and she said, to him, that the young man had been kind enough to walk her home, so the man in blue smiled to me, and I watched as he went to the elevator bank and pushed the button to her floor. The elevator doors opened and she got on, head down, and as the doors slid shut I turned, walked up the three steps, and moving rapidly, continued on my way.

There was one last thing. The clearness in her gaze as our eyes last met, just before she passed into the lobby: pain radiated from her eyes, and though she cringed from the possibility of any more pain, and therefore feared her self as the vehicle moving toward that potential, the surface she and her terror created was like an aura, was also a form of clothing, a metaphor for skin, like her soft green coat, her dark brown shoes, the pale pink, silk, scarf at her throat, even as the soft rouge on her cheeks, in futility to soften the deep lines in her face, out from behind this dress of grief, loneliness, anxiety and fear, I saw a clear-eyed determination flighting to be conscious so she could will the action she would take, for the rest of her life with others on the planet, which could only begin through the completion of her suffering. She was a small woman, in at least her late sixties, her head was slightly down, and she walked with her hands clasped before her breast, and when she had raised her griefstricken eyes to mine I saw she was terrified. But behind that veil, I saw a light of renewal.

"You'll be okay—" I had said.

Yes, she had answered, Thankyou, and had silently crossed the lobby to the bank of elevators as through a series of invisible barriers, or an invisible jungle beneath an invisible sea, fighting every step of the way for the will to patience in the gradual achievement of a conscious life with her fresh new self, and perhaps a few others.

Brave woman.

She won't make it, Blaze said. She hasn't a chance.

Why not? I asked.

Too old, he said.

Not true, I said. I've known old people who've come through hell—and besides, I saw it in her eyes.

Blaze nodded. You could be right. Maybe I'm jealous again—although you're an idealist—

From one self to another, I interrupted, we're both idealists.

I know, he nodded, putting his glasses in his pocket: the same idealist with two different names.

I put the manuscript on the desk by my typewriter, and as I went to the kitchen to make myself some coffee, I said, to end the competition, Her children will want her, and her husband will help.

Blaze appeared in the doorway and smiled. That's that cop in you, he said.

Introducing Bugs & Flap

The Stolichnaya Lecture

They had arrived a little late, because (as Dotty explained), Guy had been up all night working on a manuscript, and hadn't gotten to bed until around ten that morning. Thus he had gotten up at five or so that afternoon, and was angry at himself because he had missed the day. Anyone who knew Blaze knew how much he loved the daylight hours, and if he missed them he was apt to be irritable and impatient, even distracted. It was nine ten and he was in a bad mood. He would, I knew, be apt to take it out on us.

I went in the kitchen and laid a good jolt of cold Russian vodka over some ice, and in the spirit of the *good*

Stalin, sprinkled freshly ground pepper across the top, and inserting a stirrer from The Sherry-Netherland, I brought it to him. It was ice cold. I had returned the vodka to the refrigerator—not before I made myself a little drink, though, and as the women were drinking wine, I joined them at the table, and we sat around talking and hoping Guy Blaze's mood would change. An evening with him when he's cranky is impossible: he is the life of a party, and I knew what I was doing when I gave him what I did. Audrey and Dotty didn't, and I thought I'd see what would happen, because to be perfectly honest, I was in good spirits, and wanted him to be too. The first sign is when he licks the corners of his cherry lips.

"Christ! This vodka is good!"

I said: "Eighty proof."

"Russian vodka eighty proof?" he asked. "Since when?"

Oh oh, Audrey said, as Dotty's face darkened, and she murmured softly fasten your seatbelts as Blaze mildly mentioned he didn't know it came in eighty proof, which was a lot of baloney because he did know because we'd had it together at The Russian Tearoom. Where he gets his postcards.

The thing is that Stolichnaya eighty proof tasted just like the hundred proof, you can't tell by the taste, and the only way you know is by what goes on as you drink it, and because it tastes like the hundred, the effect is as if it was—Blaze knew by the taste, and when I said eighty, he affected surprise because the first taste said hundred, and anyway he likes to hear himself talk. I've heard him in self-conversations often, and I've heard him when he talks to himself, and sings, and hums, which is especially going on when he writes: clackety-clack, clack, clackety-clack clack, clackety-clackety clack clack ommm, he sings, clack clackety-clackety clackety clack, clack, damn! Wrong!

Wrong Blaze! Wrong *again* clack, clackclack Goddamnit—

Well, after his second drink he mentioned that because he was famous for his appreciation of brevity in speech recently some students at a certain small college had challenged him to deliver an impromptu lecture that was not only original, but interesting, and all of it under two hundred words with his deadline noon the next day. It had been near midnight when the challenge was made, which Blaze accepted, of course, and they formed a bet. He had already delivered the lecture he'd been paid five hundred dollars for, so he bet them if he lost he'd take them to supper—no spaghetti, either. If he won, they'd get him a half gallon of Popov.

He informed Audrey and Dotty, with a certain flash of eye, that he intended to deliver that brief lecture tonight, and they said Oh no.

I smiled. But he had risen to his feet, and with an inclusive gesture to the three of us, finished his drink and sat down saying Lucky, another snort for the Blaze, that fury of our collective future.

I made him a whoppa.

After the first gulp, he licked his lips lasciviously, and with his eyes beginning to shoot sparks, he stood up again, and with a mad laugh, shouted:

I AM THE FIGURE OF ELECTRICITY STORMING ABOUT MY HOUSE IN THE THUNDERBOLT OF DIS-COVERIES FINDING THE SENSE OF MY HOME—

"Guy, for Christ's sake!" cried Dotty.

MICE AND WOMEN! yelled Blaze.

He's hysterical, Audrey said, shaking her head.

Dotty said: Manic—

Manic? Blaze asked. Madness you say? with consideration being my definition for thoughtfulness, consider the mouse and those castles in the days of yore on paper: she, in all her beauty, tresses flowing, Never Underestimate the Power of a Woman, depression and war years cartoons and true madness: mere mouse? The Feminine Mystique, or in the little image another symbol of anxiety to drive her mad, oh they dance, dance, mice! and the King, ignored and irritated, steps: *bam:* down, squash, death to her relief and out it goes, a little corpse into the moat. A small plash! Not what it was, though. Monstrous in the delirium and distraction of the day as animals wander in our minds, as insects, too, crawl across the visual fields of insane fantasy and the imagination gone berserk with fear: age old images of anxiety: clues towards the OBLITER-ATION OF FEMININE ANXIETY IN THE CONQUEST OF the mere mouse oh I AM THE FIGURE OF ELECTRI-CITY STORMING ABOUT MY HOUSE IN THE THUN-DERBOLT OF DISCOVERIES FINDING THE SENSE OF MY HOME: include the actual mouse in the ecological relativity of everything: a hundred and seventy-four words. Blaze sat down with a smile.

Audrey turned to me angrily: Why do you give him the Russian, you *know* what it does to him!

Me? I asked, and turned to Dotty:

Did he eat anything today?

EAT PEAT AND BOG AND SHIT AND CLAMS! yelled Guy Blaze. He let go a really wild laugh. Tonight, he informed us, with a mad smile: I am The Joker in Carson City whereupon he began to eat an invisible— feast, I guess it was. I couldn't get the Carson City association, but he was smacking his lips, and wiping his mouth with his sleeve, muttering about the Middle Ages and a pow wow over the third person.

Dorothy asked him if he was self-conscious because he was turning fifty.

He's angry because he missed the daylight, I said.

Audrey rose from the table and went into the kitchen. The curry smelled marvelous, I joined her and told her to give Guy a little of that stuff in his last name. She smiled, and nodded. But she said she had been angry at me because she thought his lecture was good, and she would have rather heard him a little less crazy . . . she also said I was right. He is angry, she said, he used the word day twice, I think, and he is also anxious, and self-conscious, too. Dotty's right. The Middle Ages, she intelligently observed, and he's turning fifty. He's wonderful. The students must have loved it. She laughed, and kissed me on the cheek saying Help me carry some of this out, would you?

Guy Blaze was certainly hungry, he took a tablespoon full of rice and beef, and with the obvious deliciousness of dal, and mango chutney, tears were running down Blaze's cheeks, and on his second bite I rose from the table, went into the kitchen, and returned with an icy chilled bottle of Heinekin's, from which he drank thirstily.

"You're all right, Lucky," you son of a beerlush, he laughed.

The curry and the beer sobered him completely, and after supper we had a little of that cheap Spanish brandy we used to drink with Paul Blackburn, during the war. We had it in our coffee, hot and black. The women didn't.

Blaze had accepted the half gallon of Popov Vodka graciously, he told us, and had taken the students to supper anyway. Then, sitting back in his chair, he looked at Audrey.

Thankyou, dear, he smiled. That was *excellent*.

Anybody for Monopoly? Dotty asked.

It was on the trip in from Pennsylvania, I began, and Guy picked it up.

How about a sentimental story? I suggested.

61

Okay, he said, and a little—I got it! he cried. The young woman—

In the airline terminal, I said, and it was at the bar. She was sitting near the door, drinking a straight up martini with a twist of lemon.

The drink sparkled in the sunlight from the front window.

She was thin and very tall, dressed mostly in lavender. She had a flowing quality.

Like something smoky. Her fingers fiddled with the stem of the glass, and the big stone on her finger winked in the sunlight, yeah really!

You got it! he cried.

Her hair was long and silky and the color of light coffee, her skull was narrow and long (like yours, Guy), and her eyes were big, dark, and heavy lidded. She wore false eyelashes, her nose was long, and like Streisand's. Her cheeks were shallow but her lips were mmmm—

Full and painted white. Under her tan she had acne scars that were pretty deep.

Dark glasses lay beside her white handbag on the bar.

It made no difference who said what in the action at the Third Baseline Bar. Hardly a day goes by that the sports pages do not recount quote a miracle play unquote by some major leaguer.

Blaze had kept that clipping from Sports Illustrated that poet Billy McKay had given him, and the way she sat at the bar we saw her whole right leg. We were standing to her right, and almost the whole length of the bar away, but we saw her leg, the whole thing and a curve of her white panties on the outside of her thigh. Her leg looked about ten feet long—long, tan, and terrific.

Ten after two in transition: take a walk on the

Boardwalk: we had stopped in the airport terminal bar for a couple of cool ones, and.

But the sports miracle of the year (could be) was the one performed by two policemen on a 14-year-old player in a sandlot game at Irving, Tex. Their heart massage and mouth-to-mouth resuscitation was credited with saving the life of Greg Lehrer, who'd been struck by a lightning bolt while playing third base. Four dumpy businessmen in grey and brown double-breasted suits stood around the curve of the bar by us drinking Miller's.

The bartender, who was the other person in the place, was a middle-aged bald man in grey slacks, a white shirt and pink-pattern tie sitting on the edge of the sink by the beer taps, looking out the front window, and occasionally at the tall long legged smoke lady. I saw his left eye dart. Greg was knocked unconscious and lay on the ground for forty eight minutes while his two rescuers, who'd been coaching in a game nearby, worked over him (and) she raised her glass. It drifted to her lips, and she tilted and emptied it down her throat like like—Ms Jekyl, lowered her head as she swallowed, and slid the glass forward and looked down to the bartender, smiled and nodded, yes, please. Another, as he rose to his feet, cap torn to shreds, the zipper on his uniform melted.

—We'll get that, I (laughed) interrupted, curiously, and his belt buckle was so hot no one could touch it. The bartender looked at me, and then at Flap, and then down the third baseline to the tall young woman, observers on the scene reported. His legs were fused and a metal chain around his neck disintegrated.

Chance.

She nodded shyly, yes, and after looking at us again, he made the drink, took it to her and when he came back we paid him. She turned, and raising the drink to us, The youngster regained consciousness, thanks, she said, and we grinned, rather handsomely, in a hospital coma where he was told he'd been hit by a baseball. You're welcome. She sipped the drink, and turned to look out the front window.

They thought I might go into shock if I knew I'd been hit by lightning, Greg said.

The jets crouched on the tarmac beyond.

Flap said, Bugs, what do you think?

I don't quite know. I'm a little confused. I was supposed to pitch that day, but my arm was hurting me.

She doesn't look very happy, I said, and we looked at the clock on the wall, finished our drinks, tipped the bartender, and hefting our luggage as he said so long, we walked to the door passing the tall young woman with the long lovely legs, yet passing through the scent of her perfume was to move through lavender, curious, and beguiling. Take care, we said.

You too, the lavender woman said. "Thanks!" she called, to make sure, and we waved to her but she didn't see it, and as we walked along the corridor, Flap said Bugs, you saw she was crying.

I nodded, and said that's why we bought her the drink, wasn't it? Because she was upset? Did you see her legs? Jesus.

We stopped walking. Things, I remarked, happen fast.

Maybe we should have stayed with her a minute, Flap said.

What do you think? I asked.

Shall we go back? Flap asked, and as if of one mind, and perhaps even one body, we retraced our steps into the Third Baseline Bar, but no one vanishes faster than women who want to, not even fourteen-year-old kids struck by lightning. And we stood like a couple of musicians in an empty nightclub, noticing everything around the infield.

Her glass was empty, and as if on the surface of pleasant perfume, and a lavender vision with long legs, we saw details like cigars and cracker-jack, in pennies nickels and dimes to total twenty-seven cents on the bar. The dumpy double-breasted High Life business-men had left too, and the bartender was fast asleep.

It was just a little cloud passing over. In an otherwise all blue sky, and he was expected to recover. A .421 hitter.

Flap and I were cleared through the electronic beam, and after picking up our luggage, we continued down the corridor which led to our flight section.

After they had gone, Audrey said, while we washed dishes, You think it's fun when you and Guy do that, but it scares me.

Don't worry, I said, it scares us, too, only we're too daffy to take it seriously.

Lucky, look at me, she said.

I did, and she made a wry smile. It sounds like intellectual masturbation, she said, and when you two get going I can't follow you or understand you, I can't tell you apart! Dotty doesn't like it either. It seems hostile, apart, removed from us, like a secret dialogue.

I know, I said. It took us years to do it right. Okay sweetheart, I'll tell Guy. You're right, there is something spooky about it. We won't do it—when you're around.

And—when we're not?

I can't promise, I said, truthfully, because when he and I are in the bar and a certain little bell rings, off we go. But I'll try.

A certain little bell, eh? she inquired, little Spanish brandy bell in the bottom of each half pint?

65

Cadmium Orange, Rose Red, and Titanium White

1

In the double take the little doll wasn't there. Her small exquisite face was set atop the body of a giant, and her golden brown eyes peered out from above the body of a great-shouldered woman as tall as any man. The goddess voluptuous, breasts hung full. Her hips were wide, and purely animal. Her stomach was teenage taut, and when she stripped the hair between her legs was thick and long like a wild red beard. As she stood or was seated before me in full face or profile as I painted, the fire on her head was matched between her legs, and like the blonde Nana, was thick under her arms.

Her legs and thighs were tremendous, very shapely,

column-like, and imbued with force. Her feet had high arches, and were beautiful in themselves: perfect, and long with long gripping toes like her long powerful hands as gripping as the woman herself.

2

They were at the bar. Blaze and the artist Blaze had met in Berkeley (where he had lectured), whose name I didn't get—I had come in with my groceries as they were talking. I never did get his name because after he had finished his story, he had quickly said goodbye, and left the bar. Nor did I get the model's name either—but Blaze later explained that the story I had come in on was the artist's narrative of how his painting had changed from rather small controlled abstract compositions, to large broadly stroked abstract violence.

To begin with, the artist said, I sketched her, and became familiar with her whole body, and all details, as in a composition. She was shy, and aware of her body, she held her head high, she was an excellent model and a challenge I wasn't used to.

The sketches I did were terrible if I say so myself, and as she was curious, not aloof like some models, she made a point of looking at what I had done, at the end of the day. She liked what she saw, and I understood she had had some background in it herself, for the transition from the academic nude into abstract composition interested her, so it was altogether a fresh experience for me. But although I caught her small head on her massive body professionally, after the first few days, I began to be disturbed, and I asked myself if this was what I wanted.

I could have stopped right there, and had an exhibition of the drawings alone, but I changed my mind, collected them all and shelved them. In a sense they were the part of something that I was on my way to: I wanted her before me, all of her wholeness, and not only on paper but on canvas.

Consequently I did a series of quick paintings in acrylic using a variety of small brushes, and shades of color. I got her pale skin color perfectly, until around the tenth or eleventh painting when I got angry with the limitations of my own competence, and in a sense of confused disgust, I crossed my studio, took out the big brushes I had used to paint the walls, ceilings and floors of my studio with, I told her to take a break, which she did, and when she asked me what I was doing I told her I didn't know.

I have a wall on small wheels, like her in reverse, that I rolled across to where her settee was, and moving my easel into the corner, I unrolled a sheet of canvas about twelve feet long, cut the size I wanted, about six feet, and stapled it onto the mobile wall.

Then I cleared my paint table (itself mobile), and after opening my paint closet I collected all the cadmium reds I had, plus the oranges, and—suddenly angry—the two small tubes of alizarin crimson. I had thought I had more than two, but that being the way things were, I accepted it, and went into the kitchen and found a few baking pans and brought them back with me. I would begin anew in oil.

I squeezed all the paint into the pans, and after mixing in some turpentine, a good deal of it in fact, I painted the whole canvas that color: cadmium red medium, and then the whole thing cadmium red dark, but thinner on the second coat, in a certain suspicion I had lost my mind, as my heart pounded and I sensed her volume, and her freckles.

I mentioned that she lie down as if resting, which she did. A fantastic vision, let me tell you, and because I was painting her didn't mean that I didn't see her, and even though the canvas was wet and damp in different places, in a sudden obsession with her shoulders, I anxiously began slapping on square-shapes, big ones, the brush stroke about eight inches wide, in cadmium orange. I was certain I was wrong. Yet I had the sense that another force was guiding me, and while I cursed and tore my hair, stomped around my studio smoking one cigarette after another and sitting down and standing up, looking at her and then at the canvas and then back at her and then back at the canvas while she watched me what could I do, what would I do as I knew I had to do it?

Seeing red, I deepened it with ivory black, and across those bold strokes I used up all my alizarin crimson which made me feel I was right, although in effect all I had was a very deep and complicated red, I was beginning to like it.

I told her what I was going to do, and that I'd be back very soon, as I took off my apron, washed my hands in turps, then with soap and water, wiped my hands dry on a rag and went to my art supply store and bought what they had in alizarin crimson, rose reds, and cadmium oranges and returned to my studio.

She had fallen asleep.

I finished the painting.

I'd never seen anything like it, although it was definitely eclectic, and violent I admit. But the overlays of that deeply rich color combination do give the sensation she creates. I mean the volume of blood under those freckles, which had got me going, and I had to get into. You can hardly see the orange. While I was looking at it a passing interstate rig let go the air horns and she woke up, stretched, and my God what a sight! Venus wakes up, and after rubbing her eyes, made a small cry of alarm, seeing my hands, most of my arms, as well as my apron, covered with crimson—

It's okay, I said. Just paint.

She rose, put on her robe, and as she belted it she crossed the studio and looked at my painting.

"That's not me," she said.

"No," I said, likewise calm, it's all that blood under your freckles.

"I know I'm big," she said, and in the next three weeks or so I did fifteen more, some of them twelve feet long, and a couple twelve feet high, and in the fall of that year, after my exhibition and the critics saying I had gone off my rocker, I had yet made two sales, and, finally, on the basis of that, and in my inspired madness, I named them all after her, and in a numbered series beginning with the first one, I telephoned her and to make a short story shorter, took her to lunch at the Plaza (the exhibition was held in town here), and that day I spent too much money on too much champagne and caviar, but it was very nice, in fact it was wonderful, and in her quiet shy way I could see she was amused. I thanked her profusely and asked her if she would continue to model for me, to which she responded warmly yes, until January 10th, when she was getting married.

Causing her to blush, the color of which I subsequently made memorable. Forgive me.

Interlude

I met Blaze on the street, and both of us with our groceries walked to the bar, he had his laundry in the dryer, he said, and had yet to go to the post office, so if he suddenly leaps up mid-sentence, I should—

I get it, I said, and we went inside, put our groceries on the bar and sat down as Frank greeted us and we greeted him and he began to make the usual two.

As we sipped and lit up cigarettes, Blaze said he had been thinking about the boy in the body of a man.

I nodded.

Not only, he said, was I involved in him as my youth, I also think he was my other, dark self.

Yes, I nodded, and puffed on my cigarette, I think so, too, but it also holds self-destruction because you were angry at yourself for being there, plus the sexual—

Blaze held up his hand and I stopped. True, he said, but wait, friend Lucky, because as I am thinking, and remembering: I clearly recall I had an other when I was young. Does it ever stop?

No, I said. It's like wee-gee, and I spelled o-u-i-j-a: French yes, German yes.

Yes yes, Blaze smiled. But in our selves and their others are the action in the Moebius strip.

Everflow, I said, and we sipped our drinks.

Haggard Again

I had been up late meeting a review deadline, and working on a novel, so I was pretty worn out when I met Blaze, that afternoon.

One of those busybody days when I did everything I'd put off. I did the normal house-cleaning, then went to the bank to deposit a meager royalty check plus fifty for a book review I'd done for an out-of-Met magazine. I took shirts to the Chinese laundry. I went to the post office to buy some stamps, and returned some books to the library and then walked up-Met, and turned in my review to my editor. Then I came back to do the laundry and to shop for supper. I got to the bar late, near four, and

Blaze (not sober), was talking to Frank (sober).

I put the bag of laundry on the foot rail, the groceries on the bar, and pulled up a seat beside Blaze, who, turning from Frank, and glancing at me, remarked that I was late, and that I appeared weary. I nodded, as Frank made my drink, and Blaze continued his monologue. Frank nodded, gave me the drink and took my money as I sipped.

Although I hadn't had much sleep, I had had a solid breakfast plus a pastrami on rye at a Labor bar near the paper, so the little water was definitely good.

It was a beautiful day outside, cool in new solar configurations, September in July, and the brilliant sunlight angled hard off the stone and steel Metropolis walls, and poured down the avenues and into the front window like *Das Lied von der Erde:* glasses sparkling on the bar, which was crowded because it was the verge of the cocktail hour, and in the sound of Mahler in the light, I thought of my friend Asa. Ah-sa, from whom I'd received a card. From Switzerland, a few days ago.

She was on her way to Rome, where she would be for a few days. Everything was wonderful, she said, and would I please write her?

She wished I was there. She gave an address. I sipped my drink and lit a cigarette.

Blaze took a letter, or a manuscript, from an envelope, went through his usual elaborate business of taking out his reading glasses, and tilting his head back and looking down his nose over the glasses asked if I would excuse him. He had received a few poems from a student whom he had met last year, and he thought he would read them.

I nodded, weary and probably a little haggard, again, or feeling so, and suddenly fed up with washing dishes, making the bed, and sweeping the floor, which as the days vanished formed a continuity of drudgery of its own, and called for a good night's sleep to do as merely part of the day, and in reaction, as Blaze read, I fell into a reverie of Asa.

She was lovely in a disturbing way. Her skin was rich, resilient, and tawny. She had long dark hair brushed straight back to fall well below her shoulder-blades, fully revealing her broad forehead, dark and rather heavy eyebrows and very dark emotional eyes above a little button of a nose, round cheeks and her constant and helpless full-lipped pout, which with her lean and elegant figure, and style of (marching) walking (head high), generally sent guys on the streets into fits. She was about nineteen.

She had, and it was true, a heart of gold. And following the metaphor in metals, she was as tough, or as defensively hard as iron. The gold was given, but she had to acquire the iron, from a miserable childhood in a rotten city across the grey river.

She had a temper, and following her outbursts, true to her femininity, she was often shaken, and near enough to tears to bite her lower lip and say some remarkably hard words concerning guys.

Every few weeks she'd give me a call and we'd meet after work and have a few drinks together. She could hold her alcohol, and was very sweet, and very affectionate, when she'd been drinking. She got sleepy, about six hours later, and was warm and funny in the cab going home. But she didn't only drink, there had been tracks on her arm. In the past year, though, since her husband went to prison, she quit taking drugs of any sort, had cut down almost completely on drinking, and was fixing up her apartment and saving money to go overseas (she sub-let the apartment), and I had wondered how long her good self (as she called her) would last, because she had also enjoyed the pleasure of heroin, in the company of a couple of friendly savage teen-age guys she turned on with. She used to turn on with.

The day before she flew to London I took her to lunch in a place she liked, but I didn't (the bartender, a snarling pup, didn't like me, nor I him). I had broiled red snapper which was delicious, and she had London broil at which pun I smiled, and which they ruined with the gravy, which she liked.

In good spirits, that day, and as she was a good story teller, she told me what had happened on her way to the airlines office that morning, when she purchased and picked up her ticket. It had been raining, but very heavy, it had really come down, and in a fierce wind she had arrived at the office soaked clear through.

Her life is and it was, an adventure. She reached across the table and took my hand saying, as she swallowed and looked at me: I was walking or trying to walk, down the street in that wind and rain with my dress almost up to my neck and me trying to hold it down and keep my umbrella up it's a stupid fuckin' umbrella, when I saw one of those (she chuckled) *third world* types.

Her eyes flashed, as she smiled.

I laughed.

Well, she continued, that son of a rice paddy purses his lips and starts sucking at me, and I got so *fuckin'* mad! I lowered my umbrella, closed it, ran at him and took a swing at him—he was *big*, too, with heavy shoulders, a lotta muscle, and he ducked, so I swung at him again and missed, I was cussing to match the wind and I kicked him

78

in his stomach. I got *long* legs—you know—(I nodded, and sighed) (she laughed), and the dude comes AT me!

Wow, I said.

Yeah! she cried, he started coming at me, and I was really scared, and started to back up, but—and she looked out the window at the street over my shoulder, then met my eyes. She tilted her head towards me and curled her lips:

"Then I got *mad*."

And out of the storm, another guy appeared, just as she swung her umbrella at the first guy, cussing him and screaming that he let her alone—*a-lone*, she then hit him over the head with her umbrella and the other guy stepped inbetween them, she turned and walked down the street so wet, furious and frustrated she forgot to thank the guy who had helped her. This is good, she said. "Why don't you like this place?"

They don't like me, I said.

Why? she asked, and laughed. That was funny (somebody else getting it for a change). She had a teen-age laugh that was amusing in itself.

I said they don't like me because I am what I am, and that's what I am.

"You and Popeye," she said. "Can I have a bite of your salad?"

I slid it across to her, and as she took some, I realized the real reason was because I was with her, and that they were jealous. But it was also true they didn't like me, period, as in the Lorenz doctrine: I had come into their neighborhood (territory), and I was different.

With a forkful of greens before her lips she asked if she could have another drink. It was, after all, a big city lunch, so I said sure, and she fell into thought and on a slow glide, didn't say anything.

Then, and a little desperately, she asked: *"Why?"*

"Tell me," she added. "You're smart. I want to know —please," she pleaded.

"You're the classic girl guys fall for," I said.

She closed one eye slowly, and tilting her head to her right, asked, "Yeah?"

I nodded yes, and she said Classic, eh? and smiled. I smiled inwardly and said, with a light shrug, They're unconscious, and helpless in the face of you. You awaken something in them they never knew they had, or dreamed of.

"Yeah?" She liked that.

Um hum, I smiled.

Then suddenly serious, and then again a bit desperately, as in a confession of mystery: "But Lucky, it's *everywhere!*"

"Yes," I said. "So are you to them." I said, further, and warmly, You're something that was once lovely everywhere, to them. In them, I thought.

"But I'm a woman!" she cried, and I saw she was hurt.

"To put it mildly," I said. "For which conscious *men*, not these boys, will love you. These ghoul-children in their steady sleepwalk can't. You remind them of something that maybe—way back—was of beauty, pride, security, but which yet threatens, and they're frightened: loveliness frightens them, and they'll mock it, hurt it, and even destroy it, as if by being it has betrayed them, like mother, and in their unconscious rage they would fuck and furiously masturbate, rather than—"

"You mean I'm their *Mother?*" Incredulous.

"Beauty is everybody's Mother," I said.

She made a slit-eyed smile, and said, "They'd fuck me rather than see me."

I nodded.

And youth looks free, I said.

"So that's why," she whispered, "that they beat those kids on the peace marches."

80

I nodded.

She swore, and frowned, and in awe, said: "Gimme that once again in brief so I can remember."

I did. I also got us another drink. The waitress was hassled, hard-boiled and typically pleasant-faced when she smiled, which she was too busy to do, much of, but she did when I thanked her, rather shyly, for a fact, and though she was middle-aged, her calves were hard and shapely as she moved swiftly to the next table. Asa and I toasted Europe.

We drank our drinks and smoked cigarettes, and talked.

It was very nice, and even.

When we left, the sun was out and the city smelled clean. She had fallen silent as we'd finished, and I'd paid the bill, left a tip, helped her into her coat and had received a quick look, so I let her do it herself, and we went outside. I flagged down a cab, and before she got in she thanked me for the lunch and then came close to me, face up. I caught her in a quick embrace, and we held each other close, and kissed. She drew back briefly, put her hand on my cheek and said I'll write you, will you write me? she asked softly. I will indeed, I said. She looked up at me, and her dark and youthful emotional eyes were wide and glittering. Lucky, she said.

You're a nice guy. I really like you.

I said: You're wonderful. Have a good flight.

She laughed (she knew), and I opened the rear door of the cab. She ducked expertly—tail first—inside, and after she pulled her legs in I closed the door, and we looked at each other.

As it drove away she turned, and waved to me from the rear window.

I held up my hand and smiled.

So you knew Alicia Peabody? I laughed, suddenly.

I most certainly did, Blaze answered, shifting in his seat. She was a dear friend.

His eyes got a distant look, and he murmured: Beautiful creature!

I looked out the front window of the bar, and in a figure of irritation realized I'd be sorry if I didn't, and hadn't, known better, so I said something to that effect to him.

Blaze said, Hum!

I sipped my drink.

The Things We Did Last Summer

It's been my good fortune to have known and loved several truly beautiful and intelligent women, most of whom will be friends for life. I can, like Steve Canyon, gaze back down on that long and winding road and meet them again, and again fall in love. For example there is the photograph of Alicia Peabody. Framed, in back, on the wall by the window that opens onto the fire escape. She is glancing up, and has a big grin. She had cut her hair (she wrote), and afterwards went into a whole thing about it, realizing that she shouldn't have, but, I told her, be patient and it will grow back. Which helped, but not much, and anyway she was as lovely in short hair as she was in long, which I also told her, but that too didn't help much. But in any event it was easy to see why Marlon liked her, as well as I.

He had left her little notes. Tender ones, and as his handwriting is small, so too his signature, but the message was clear and bright: Where are you? I was here! And where were you?

Talk about competition!

Somewhere around those days when she received those notes she mentioned—briefly, that she had been friends with Jackson Pollock in Provincetown, and I had that curious fenced-in feeling, like when we went to hear Miles, and he faced and played to her. I mean, well, I was much younger then and of course so was Alicia, and I was extremely jealous. A fact she found amusing, irritating, and in that order, strictly bothersome.

"Oh why WORRY!" she would cry.

Well, I thought, if you perhaps were me you might worry too! Who can help it? But women tend to think literally, an important fact to remember, and as she was certainly my match in brains, she, well, actually she was smarter. True. Smarter'n me, and this *if you were me* business completely baffled her. She went into gales of laughter because she knew how I thought, what I thought, and when I was thinking what it was that I was.

"Not again," she would say. Really, you're too much.

But, like most women, she intensely and seriously disliked being baffled, because she suspected it was (and it was) trickery of some sort, because for example I was being dishonest with myself and wouldn't simply admit I was jealous. Yes, you're Goddamned right I am, so watch out, catchya with another man, that's the end.

"Watch out who?" she asked.

Oh her eyes would twinkle, and she got that smile which made my stomach sink and my legs go all wobbly and my blood hot hot hot, and hotter.

"Well?"

You, I thought. You watch out, but then! I realized what she meant, because what she was saying was to me, in a question: No, Lucky, you watch out. And what the (oh!) *dazzling* smile meant was she was amused because she was very irritated: You're the one who's jealous. Not me!

Of course she watched me figure all this out, and I mean it was tough going. Which showed on my face as clearly as Zapata on the screen, as I repeated, in my special density, Watch out *who?* Who, what?

"Watch out who," I said out loud. She saw I was getting angry. I began walking around the apartment, getting angrier, clenching and unclenching my fists, etc. Snorting. You get it.

Then I got it.

She sighed, and made a face. "At last," she said.

"Yeah," I said. Me.

Yeah, she said. "You."

Me being jealous I should watch out, I said, and she was smarter'n me.

Yes yes yes yes *yes*, she said, and I saw a gleam of anger in her eyes. "You," she said. "Not me."

You, right, I admitted. I know, and she frowned and made her lips into a thin tight line, and cried,

"Why does it always take you FOREVER?"

She went into the kitchen, opened the refrigerator and took out a plum, washed it, and ate it. I was standing in the doorway, feeling pretty stupid—and angry—watching her. She looked at me, and whispered,

"Don't look at me like that."

"Like what?" I said. What a sap.

She lowered the plum, and looked at me: "You are impossible."

She brushed by me and went into the living room,

and as she went through the doorway she threw her hands up and yelled,

"IMPOSSIBLE!"

Well good God, she was right! And I wouldn't admit that I was such a sap, and in my anger at myself I was (this is what, and how, it happens), objective of her. Separate from, looking at her like I'd look at a painting, which is to say no matter how lovely, still an object.

But, in the game of it—and a bad game it was, for me especially—that looking was a real way to get her attention. Or goat. It's a flat, lazy ox-like expression. A dull look. And it can mean he can't handle his anger at himself, so he swings his gaze onto her.

"I'm sorry," I said, a trifle suddenly.

She sighed, and then sighed deeply, and said, in irritation: "Yes, oh yes I know, but you *know* I hate that. And yet you do it! You know it's my job to be looked at and you know how I hate it anyway, but you still *do* it." She chuckled angrily, seeing the embarrassed beast (me).

"YOU!" she yelled, exasperated: "you're impossible. Listen, if you *want* me, or want to talk to me, or want my attention, then say my name, but DON'T LOOK AT ME like *that!*"

It really scared her. It sent her into an uncontrollable self-consciousness, an intense self-doubt rose up and became coupled with her complicated guilt structure, and sent her reeling, it hurt, boy it hurt her, and when she begged me not to look at her like that, it was a plea for refuge from a storm she knew by heart but couldn't handle, and it was in fact the one thing she hated most of all, and she had to summon her total anger not to fight me, but to fight that wave, that drowning violence beautiful women often suffer: the certainty of worthlessness.

It hit her swiftly and as hard as a hammer, and could knock her senseless.

The oxen look on.

"I'm sorry," I said again. "Really, sweetheart."

"I know you are, of course you are, but," and she lowered her head a little, fighting for control, and she said, softly: "You don't know what it's like."

"I know I don't," I admitted. "I don't even know what I'm doing, or what the hell's going on here, but I'm damned sorry and won't do it again, I promise. I'm an idiot."

"You're not an idiot," she said clearly, "and that's the problem, because you're so—" she looked at me, eyes questioning: "you're so intelligent," she finished.

I nodded, ashamed.

Tableau.

Come, she was thinking: sit by me. Hold my hand. I did.

"Don't say anything," she said. "Please."

I won't, I thought, sending the thought to her as I took her hand and sat on the floor before her, as she sat in her favorite (rocker) chair, by the window which opened onto the fire escape. There was a little table by the chair, with purple, scarlet, and blue pansies in a small white ceramic bowl. On a blue and white checked cloth. In the soft scent of her perfume, a pale ray of sunshine fell on her wrist, as our eyes met, and held unblinking.

We had a quiet lunch.

That afternoon we went to a movie, shopped, and came home, made a great simple supper, had a little fight, made up, went to bed and read until we fell asleep.

Are you kidding? she had asked, angrily.
Who, me? I asked, and then said no.

All right, she said, but I don't like the tone of your voice.

I don't either, I admitted (angry at myself), and we sort of glared at each other. She said something under her breath, reached out, picked up the paper and started looking through it murmuring a little louder, you're really something. Why do you even talk to me?

Because I—well, I love you, I said. Why are you so critical of me?

If you love me, can't you think what you say before you say it? Can't you consider me? I have to hear it, you know.

I'm always considering you, I said. Probably too much.

Well there you go! she cried. That's it! Stop considering me then!

I narrowed my eyes, and looked at her. I don't, I said, altogether get that.

Oh you're impossible, she smiled angrily, can't you see? Consider yourself, then.

First?

Always, she said firmly, and set her jaw saying: The self you consider is the self that considers me.

I nodded. Would I ever get there? I said well I am sorry, and you know—

She lowered the paper to her lap and gave me an exasperated look, as she said but you're always sorry afterwards, after you say these things.

I said, But isn't it possible that I can be wrong? Just-plain-wrong, without all this special treatment?

She threw the paper onto the table, jumped out of the rocking chair and faced me: Yes! she cried, *but it is you*, and can't you break this flamboyant habit and remember that *you're* speaking to me, I mean isn't it clear, really? that I'm not just-plain-anybody, and that you aren't either?

I know that, I said, defensively.

But you don't *think*, she said, and was getting upset.

I said. Okay. That's true. You're right. I do say things without thought to you, and it is true I say foolish things also, that I wouldn't say to myself, but maybe it's because you don't know, down deep, the effect you have on me.

She sat down, slowly, and looked out the window. Then she nodded, and sighed, drew a hand across her forehead, and turning in the chair, she looked up at me.

"You're right," she said.

Then she was standing with her back to me, which gave her the margin of alone-ness she loved. Then she turned, and faced me. She came to me, and gazing seriously upwards into my eyes, her brow clear and her eyes steady, she said,

I know I unsettle you. I don't mean to. You know I don't.

I nodded.

I'll try and stop. I'm sorry I'm so impatient.

She reached up and clasped both hands around my neck. She parted her lips so I could see the tips of her white teeth, and catch the clean scent of her natural breath (she didn't smoke or have commercially scented breath). She said: I know it's asking a lot, but once again you must understand me, and it is true that maybe I expect too much from you and of you, but it's because I love you Lucky, and you too should know the effect you have on me. You have a terrific effect on me. Lucky was not my name then.

I put my hands on her shoulders, and we looked in each other's eyes tenderly, in friendship and affection. I nodded, and said yes. I know.

We stood for a moment, then, cheek to cheek, in a little embrace.

She was a floor model for a ho hum exclusive so-called agency, and she liked it *okay*, but not much more. The money was nice, so she put up with it and she did watch her diet carefully.

But she got looked at all day long. Five days a week. So when she came home she wanted to do what she wanted to do, her self.

But I was working on my first novel then, and her self was more than interested in what I was writing.

Women enjoy knowing things, especially what they want to know, and the form of their wanting to know can appear in an intense and generally appealing curiosity which is famous, and when her curiosity is satisfied, she'll go on with what she was doing anyway, happier for the discovery, and Alicia Peabody wanted to read my manuscript.

And she could be *most* beguiling. Any man who is any kind of person at all knows that a curious woman who happens to be a very intelligent knockout will get her way —or else. It isn't funny, it's like being tickled, she laughs, and gets up close to you and says little things aw c'mon in her special little voice otherwise heard for a far different purpose and in a much more intimate situation. Ah, well.

Ah, well.

So she would come from work, take off her job clothes, put on something comfortable, make herself a cup of tea, come and sit with me and ask me what I did all day, and after I'd told her, she was pleased and said that that was good and she looked forward, some day, to reading it.

She knew writers don't show *anybody* their first draft, and as I had finished the first draft and was doing the correcting and re-writing, I was in a tough spot. She was a real fan of mine, she loved my work, and as the weeks went by I saw her curiosity was making real inroads on her patience. She'd read some of my stories, essays, and followed my reviews (I was just starting, then), and as she wrote poems herself, enjoyed the theatre and films, and loved to read good books, we had a lot to talk and fight about. So far she had shown restraint, but then as sure as Christmas, her curiosity got the better of her, and she began to go into action.

Her eyes got brighter, and her smile turned into a laugh. She chuckled, and sat in my lap. She put her arms around me, and said things like Hi, work hard today?

I nodded. Still on the first draft—

"Oh not *still!*" she said, irritated. She fought back anger, and scowled, stroking my cheek. "Why can't you finish—one! Just *one* chapter for me. *Please*, Lucky." Then she smiled, warmly, beautifully. "For me. Is it about me?"

We laughed. She working her charms (and she had some charms to work!), but I had to be honest, yet diplomatic. So I told her to be patient, it was just a little more and then I could show her a chapter. I told her I wanted to show it to her, and wanted to tell her about the whole book, but it was so well written (?) that if she'd be patient a little longer, it would be worth it. Anything before then would spoil it. All of which was true, I had to be honest, directly honest and yet fair to myself, etc., too, but I had to keep her away in a way that would keep her happy, because her unfulfilled curiosity made her angry and frustrated, and it was dreary being with her. And a hard atmosphere to write in. She too had problems, fighting her sense of vengeance, and her impatience, and it honestly took the two of us to make it work, which we did.

So when I handed her a completed chapter typed neat and clean, her eyes widened, and glowed, and with the manuscript in hand, she went into the bedroom, closed the door part way, relaxed on the bed, bit into an apple (we kept a bowl of fruit at bedside), and began to read.

I heard her murmur things like *wow*, gee *whiz*, and when she finished she rested a while, thinking about it. Then she took a nap, woke, read it again, got up, made us both a cup of tea and returned my manuscript to me with the formality of R. E. Lee handing over the sword to U. L. Grant.

"This," she said, "is great. You're wonderful," and, which she enjoyed doing, she put her arms around my neck and kissed me. She also liked to sit in my lap. She liked to climb, too. She'd climb up and sit on my lap, like a baby. What a baby. With one arm around my shoulder, and her head against my cheek, I brought her against me, and with our free hands, we clasped hands, and sat together, often until she fell asleep, and evening became night. And night became etc.

She's overseas these days, teaching alien children in an American Empire grade school.

There was a fellow named Ty whose last name I never knew. I met him once, in the hallway, as he lived on the floor beneath hers. He played trumpet, he was white, and Miles was an influence, and could Ty play! He was also in love with Alicia Peabody, and I could tell, because when he practised, he played the kind of songs she liked the way she liked to hear them, and as our tastes were similar, what he played was wonderful the way he played, we generally stopped what we were doing to listen.

He's in love with you, isn't he? I asked her.

She grinned, made a little laugh and said yes, in the tone of voice that said isn't that a pretty button!

There was one song that he played often, and which I never tired of. Whenever I hear it, I think of her, and see her wonderful face before me. He used an open horn, and played it clear, wide, and tenderly perfect: *The Things We Did Last Summer*. I'll be there, sitting cross-legged on the rug with her in silence, listening to him, playing to her, as our eyes met as we smiled. How could anything so right go wrong?

Her father died, and she went home to take care of her mother. I told her not to go, that she must live her own life. But she went anyway, and eleven years later telephoned me to tell me I'd been right.

Audrey had answered the telephone. Well.

This is foolish talk.

Alicia was very sensitive, and that probably means she was too sensitive.

It was important that everything be where she wanted it, not a thing to be moved unless she moved it, or changed unless she changed it, and one day she remarked she thought it would be nice if the floor in the shower was blue.

So when she went to work the next morning, I went out and bought a half pint of high gloss midnight blue, returned and after adding white and some yellow, I painted the shower floor in a home-made Aegean blue. It looked swell, and late in the afternoon when it had dried, I gave it a second coat, and when she came home she was furious, and actually shocked when I happily showed her.

"OH!" she cried, "Won't you *ever* learn?"

Learn? I said, "I thought you wanted it blue!"

She pursed her lips, sighed, and looked at me. "What," she said, "you can never seem to learn is there are ways and whens."

I said nothing.

She nodded. "Yes," she said, "and I wanted to take a shower!"

"It'll be dry by tomorrow morning, and—"

"There *are* no tomorrows, can't you see?"

I was puzzled, and certainly irritated.

"I wanted today," she explained, sadly. "I know I'm being childish," she admitted, "but I wish that you would have told me."

"I thought I'd surprise you."

"Oh I know you did," and with a frown and a couple of amusing curses, she went into the bedroom, closed the door, took off all her clothes and lay down for a nap.

There was nothing I could do but continue doing what I'd been doing anyway, my novel was coming along, I was enthusiastic, so I made myself a cup of tea, and returned to work. A couple of hours later I heard her moving around, and soon she came out of the bedroom, dressed in her shabby darling robe, and barefoot went into the kitchen and began making supper.

It was a quiet meal, and afterwards we washed the dishes and cleaned up, and while she wrote letters I watched television. Then we went to bed and read before we slept. The next morning I heard her humming in the shower. I took a towel, and stood outside the shower stall, she turned off the water, drew back the curtain and stepped out onto the bath mat as I handed her the towel. She smiled and thanked me, and then laughed rather musically. Her eyes sparkled as she quickly dried herself making little melodic noises, and when she was completely dry she came to me, put her arms around me, kissed my heart, raised her hands up around my neck and her face up to mine and said, seriously:

"Thanks for painting it. It's a gorgeous color, and it reminds me of you."

I kissed her, and stepping back a little, held her wonderful breasts in my hands, and we stood, looking at each other. Me dressed, she stripped. She sighed.

"Well, I have to go to work."

I nodded, reluctantly, and she kissed my hands, and planted a fierce one on my lips, lest I forget, and with a flashing glance, went into the bedroom to dress. I made myself a cup of coffee. She could dress swiftly, when she wanted to, and as the ritual of what-she-would-wear was the beginning of her transformation into her professional self, the fully clothed woman who emerged ready for work was slightly different than the one who had just stepped out of the shower. A fact I always noticed—how could I help it? Like a little joke, she mimed the face of a floor model, dropped it, smiled angrily, waved and went to the door as I said, from my desk, "So long, sweetheart," she opened the door, and again smiling to me, left, her cheerful words floating behind her:

"Work well!"

I heard her footsteps to the elevator, and spiritually I walked with her.

She'd go out and get a cab. On the corner. Body alert, awake, her lovely legs bare to a (white) pleated mini-skirt, and her thrilling tummy and unfettered breasts under a pink shirt open two buttons down.

Auburn hair in pigtails, her bright face to the sky. Rain perhaps?

She smiled and I saw her dimples. The darling kind, and her keen brown eyes fell on mine, through the city. I kissed—my spirit kissed her shapely lips that, albeit were critical! knew how to nibble.

"It's good to see you," she said when she got home. "And it's good to be home. Bad day at work. I want to lie down."

She went into the bedroom, stripped and lay flat out on the bed. The door was open, and as she slept I glanced in, as I sat at my desk.

She had undone her pigtails, and her hair fell across

the yellow pillow. Her face, and body, in repose, was a dream.

I showed restraint.

And continued typing the clean copy of another chapter. At the point when the shadow reached the base of the chimney on the rooftop across the way, I made a cup of tea, and woke her with the cup in my hand. She was a leetle peeved, she loved her sleep! I set the tea on the table by the bowl of fruit, and left the room.

I had a cup of tea myself, and a cigarette, and as I typed I heard her sipping and puttering around, and then she came out, barefoot in short pants and a faded blue work shirt. She came straight to me, and as I pushed my chair back from my desk, she climbed up and got settled in my lap, put her arms around me, and we kissed. She nibbled a little, and then got serious and with her hands on the back of my neck, too, so did I, I ran my hand up under her shirt. Her back arched and her whole body stretched against me as we kissed passionately.

With a dip of her shoulder she unbuttoned the shirt, and it tumbled to her waist as she raised and freed the other arm, and after we embraced and I felt her breasts as we kissed, she got off of my lap, and standing before me like Venus stepping out of water, she had stepped out of her short pants, and effortlessly shed her little panties. She stood before me, facing me, looking directly into my eyes with an intense, hard yet trembling expression. I rose, stripped swiftly, and we looked at each other, breathing deeply. She came into my arms with a low hum in her throat, and kissed my chest, my throat, my neck under my ear, and then met my lips, as both my hands were on her body, and both her hands on mine, too, very hot, and demanding our bodies were as we entered the bedroom. She clung to me, and as we lay on the bed I kissed her lips and put my arms around her and my hands under her head and she embraced me completely, wrapped her legs around mine, and on first contact, she sighed and murmured something, and moved to let me go all the way in, and when I did, we relaxed completely, and made little moves, she mostly, so we could settle to it, which we did, and then, to guide her into it, I began to make my moves, and feeling her respond, I smiled, and looked down on her. Her eyes opened, and met mine. She smiled too, hugged me tight, as we kissed as with my right hand I felt her body. She loved it, she really loved it, and then I stopped, put both my arms around her so that my hands gripped her shoulders, and we moved, slowly, slowly, as the pleasure in our loins began to tingle, and then zig zag and we held each other, my lips at her right ear and her lips at my left ear, as she sighed heavily, and deeply, and then she began to pant, and in the sustained rise, she opened her throat as I slowly, in full power, moved all the way in and then moved back out as her back arched she came to get me and I slowly went in and held, and as she gripped me and followed me I backed out a little, and then I went in with everything as she began to hum and sing and shout as I held and came as she shouted and continued to love, fiercely, pulling me to get all of it down to the last drop.

We briefly napped. We woke and had tea together in bed, in warm silence, and when the tea was finished and we lay in ease, I put my hand on her cheek, slid it down her neck, over her shoulder, down around and around her breasts as she gasped down her tummy too and around to her fabulous bottom as she began to kiss me. We changed position, and she kissed my chest and my tummy too, and then she began to nibble, and raising her head and giving me a savage glare, she went down further, and nibbled some more. She nibbled at my balls. I felt my stomach flip as she left there and began nibbling up my shaft, and when she began to use her lips and tongue both, and she began to settle into position, I had to wrench her head away which caused·her eyes to blaze in anger, but I wanted to fuck, and she whispered, in a soft hiss, What are you doing? I'm going to fuck, I answered. But, she said, as she came to me and I moved on top of her and she put her legs around me, and her arms, too, But *I like that!*

So do I, I said, though not so much as this with you, and she was irritated, briefly, and then we were both silent and relaxed as we very easily found our rhythm, and in a friendly familiarity which lasted until it changed or rather until we forgot, the sun went down, streetlights winked on and people took off their sunglasses to see what was going on in the world. Alicia began to pant, and then to hum and sing and *really* shout.

How could anything so right go wrong?

"You should teach," she said, one night, after reading an essay I had written on what I thought education was.

Flattery was not an unknown way to get to me, so I told her I'd show her something *really* good, and I leafed through my novel, found a page, and showed it to her.

"This is why I don't want to teach," I said.

Because you want to write.

I nodded, and she read it.

"Oh," she said, "that's when we had that *awful* fight!"

I said yes, and her eyes flew right and left down the typed page. I let her turn to the next page, and then gently took it away from her as she greedily read and me saying no no, no reading first draft.

"But you remember everything we said!" she cried, and taking my face in her hands, she looked into my eyes searching: "There is one thing I want to ask, and I want you to tell me. A Yes or no answer will do it. Okay?"

"Okay," I agreed.

"Did you write how grateful I was?"

I nodded, making a mental note—be sure and include how grateful she was. She stood up (she had been sitting with me by my desk), and she put her hand on my cheek. "Good," she said. "Because, to add to your list of facts, another thing women like is a man who likes himself, and isn't afraid to say so."

She knelt at my feet, and put her right hand on my knee and looked up at me. She was beautiful.

"Thanks, Lucky."

I kissed her hand, and she rose, and crossed to her rocking chair, sat down, looked in the table drawer for her sewing kit, found it, and taking some blue jeans from a basket I realized that at long last she was going to patch them. And while I read some essays by Charles Lamb, I occasionally glanced over as she intently worked. The patch was of blue polka dots on a green field, and would fit on the seat of her pants which covered the part of her bottom I liked best, the under part, just before it meets the leg, which I knew very well, and felt a continuing and extraordinary affection for.

Sensing me watching, she looked up. Attractive and darling in her granny glasses:

"One thing I don't understand," she said. "Your book reads so rapidly I don't have the sense of the action being described."

"I like the description spoken," I said.

"I'm not used to it," she said, candidly, " but I like it." She chuckled.

And I laughed.

"There you go again," she scowled over her glasses: "what's funny?"

"You amused me," I said.

She made a thin smile, and said that the surface was transparent, to which I nodded. How was that possible when the writing is deep?

I don't know, I said. "I do, but can't say it."

"Oh you know," she said. "I know you know."

"I try and write up—upwards."

She lowered her sewing, and looked at me. "I know what you mean," she smiled slyly. "You write from consciousness up!"

Because consciousness is the surface striven for—

"True," I said, to her bright expression. "And that's terrific. Thanks, sweetheart."

She grinned, and winked: "You *betcha!*"

I rose from my desk to kiss her. She had just come home from work.

"No, don't touch me," she said angrily and wearily, and avoiding my eyes she crossed into the living room taking off her coat. I went back to work. The late afternoon sun streamed through the window, and somewhere I heard music.

I heard her sigh, and as I typed, out of the corner of my eye I saw her cross into the kitchen and begin to make some tea. I wondered what was going on, and she said, from the kitchen, reading me,

That isn't it.

What isn't.

"Never mind," she answered. Let me rest a bit.

I turned in my chair, and looked into the kitchen, and said, "If you want to talk later, you can. I've worked well today, and I feel receptive."

She smiled vaguely, and yet frowned again, and I saw she was tied up inside herself. Then she said,

"I'm going to a play with John tonight. You met him, and liked him, so there's no cause to be—"

"But," I said, feeling anger, "we were going to the movies."

She made a pinched face, and was immediately angry. "Well I forgot, and it's too late."

Too late for me, I thought, jealously.

She read me, and cried: "Oh you're impossible! John doesn't have a phone, and you *know* it!"

I nodded. I forgot that, I admitted to myself, and I stood up saying, "I don't care what you do, if you tell me beforehand—"

She looked at me: "Who do you think you are?"

I said, "Don't you know?"

She turned, and walked through the living room and into the bedroom, and I heard her jump onto the bed. I followed her, and stood by the bed, over her. She was lying on her back, feet crossed, hands flung out and eyes closed. She said,

"I'm wrong. I know it. I forgot. I'm sorry. What," she said, flatly, "shall we do."

"Call the theatre and have him paged when he gets there, and tell him the truth. Set it up for tomorrow night. He'll understand."

"The movie changes tomorrow," she said.

"Movie?" I said.

She rolled over away from me, murmuring something, and for a moment I thought my mind was slipping. Then I realized somehow she had gotten John and me mixed up, so I made a peaceful offering, saying if she wanted me to call the theatre I would and she sighed and then said okay.

She had arranged to meet him at ten to seven in the lobby, and at ten to seven I phoned the theatre and paged him, he was there and he answered and I told him what was going on. He said okay, swell, and I said she'd meet him tomorrow evening, same circumstance, and they could see the play and he laughed and said that'd be fine, which I reported to her, and it was a rather dense, tense and difficult silence Alicia and I shared over evening tea, together. We then went to the movie, which was good. But we liked it for different reasons, so I stayed silent as she talked, and when we got home she was furious. When we got into the living room she turned on me and said I was hopeless.

"Well look, sweetheart," I said, "what the hell is it?"

"Don't sweetheart me, you didn't even see what they were *doing!*"

"Yes I did," I said. "But what I liked was the script, I thought it was—"

"Yes, but can't you see other things? Didn't you see how they moved?"

"Yes, and I liked that, and it fit with what they said—"

"Well, John says—"

John? I interrupted. "John said what, when."

She laughed. "Oh you."

So *that* was it! She wanted to see the movie with John! And because John was an actor, she turned the movie into a play! And arranged to see a *play* with him tonight! She'd switched us around, wanting to see the play with me! Why didn't she tell me? I was getting angrier.

"Why didn't you tell me you wanted to see the movie with John?"

"Oh PLEASE PLEASE stop!" she yelled.

I took a step toward her, and she smirked: "You're pretty sharp tonight. Unusually so."

"I told you I'd worked well, and was receptive."

Yes, her eyes said, guiltily, so you did. Well. But then

I saw she was angry at some tangling thing, and wanted to wrestle with it, so I said,

"Look—"

"There are ways I like to be with John, and ways I like to be with you—"

The rage-eruption came in a wave, and in the instant I'd taken another step toward her, and I said, between my teeth:

"You're doing this deliberately. What ways."

"Ways," she said, with a secret smile, and narrowed eyes. She took a step toward me, opened her eyes wide, and gazing into mine seriously and at length, without a trace of a smile, she said: "Hit me."

God *knows* I wanted to, but in my fury I saw her eyes glaze, and then strangely clear, and become bright, then extremely bright, and wide, and she turned her face higher to me and her eyes blazed: "Hit me, Lucky," she said, and I stood there, my right hand in a fist, as I looked down on her and then thankfully I got it, she had hated herself all day and had wanted to avoid me, and seek distraction with her friend John, so I said to her, "No," and advanced on her, "I won't hit you," and I was still furious, and wondering why she had hated herself that day and why avoid me? Probably meaning she hated herself for wanting to need me when in her cycles, hate came up top, I said, and with no humor whatsoever,

"But I'll spank your ass if you don't get into the bedroom, and lie down!"

She laughed!

I reached out to grab her shoulders to shift her body towards the bedroom, but she dodged away, turned, and from just a few feet away showed me a face of utter ugliness, hatred and fury as she laughed, making a twisted loathsome witch's mask, sticking her tongue out at me, and said in a little girl's voice: *"Fuck you!"* ran into the bedroom, slammed the door and locked it. By the sound, she flung herself onto the bed, and I heard her laugh, and laugh, and as sure as these things happened to her in the first place, she began to cry.

I half expected a tantrum, but as I stood there, her tears subsided, and then all was quiet. My God, what a face she had made!

Well, great, she's resting. I took a blanket and pillow, and sat outside on the fire escape while it got later and later. The night was very clear and the stars were bright. I leaned back, smoking a small Italian cigar, and listened to somebody's record of A Slow Boat to China.

I was happy, in a sense, and I must have dozed, because the first conscious sense I had was of her scent, and then I felt her touch.

"Want some strawberries?" she asked.

I looked at her, dim in the shadow beyond, on the inside of the apartment, and answered yes, and I felt her touch.

Wonderful, I smiled.

Let's sit for a while, she suggested, and then take a shower together, okay?

Perfect, I said, so she got a pillow, I moved over, and she sat beside me, took a puff off my cigar, murmured that it was good, and I put my arm around her and she snuggled close. We stayed like that for a while, and then she snuggled very close, put her head on my shoulder and I rested my cheek on the top of her head, and we listened to Miss Brown To You, and sort of dozed a little. On the lovers' signal we rose together, went inside taking the stuff with us, stripped in the living room, took a shower together, and had some strawberries too. The shower had been pretty neat.

We read until we fell asleep. Fortunately we both tended to sleep deeply, so our sleep was sound, and rejuvenating, which is why we were so cheerful when we woke, and enthusiastic at breakfast, and for a woman who had a nine-to-five five day a week job, and who really loved to sleep (I never missed being inwardly delighted when once awake) she jumped into it, which meant to me, that at bottom she loved to be conscious best of all.

It was on one of those mornings that we both got a surprise. There was a knock on the door, and when Alicia opened it she made a cry, and ran into the arms of an old friend (it was quickly explained) who had returned, or was returning, from many years in Europe, and as she, Alicia's friend, had no money and no place to stay, it was decided that she stay with us, and that was how it ended.

The woman, Alicia's friend, was in bad emotional shape, and needed to talk with a friend more than anything, so seeing that Alicia and the woman were extremely close, I realized that my presence would interfere, and in spite of weak and slightly guilty requests to stay, I got a small apartment mid-Metropolis, near Red Indiana Place, in fact, and continued to work on my novel. I visited Alicia once in a while, and she visited me, too, but I saw she had found an alternative, and was in fact happy. It was true that she missed me, and certainly true that I missed her, an understatement it would take too many words to stress, in fact, but it being the case, I accepted, although it hurt because I had gotten so used to her. I believe she had gotten used to me, but I don't think she was sure she wanted to, and thus her attitude toward me changed when we were together, and as the weeks went by the visits became less and less, though I did notice a certain despondency in her gaze.

I finished my novel, and through a writer I knew then, I found an agent who sold it for me, for a modest if not miserable advance.

Thus, the following spring, it was published, and

there was a small party to which I invited Alicia (she didn't come), and afterwards, in a good mood, though wondering why she hadn't come (she had been pleased the book had been accepted), a group of writers and editors took me to a restaurant for supper, and while having drinks before, at our table, I noticed a fellow coming through the crowd toward us and looking at me. I had known him a few years back, and he was a creep then and last I heard still is, but he wanted to shake my hand, wish me good luck on my book, meet my editor and make the contact, and tell me he had seen Alicia Peabody at the Vanguard, earlier in the evening listening to Ornette with a couple of guys. My friends, as I went into shock, rose from the table and hustled the creep from the restaurant, and returned to join me and help calm me down. But the thunderbolt, or the great wave had struck and I was spinning, and being tossed around, so I left the restaurant, made my way to Alicia Peabody's apartment, and knocked on her door, envisioning her in bed with some other fellow. There was no answer, so I knocked again, and as I was near tears, again I knocked, and still not hearing any motion inside the apartment, I put my fist through the wooden panel of the door, reached in, shot the bolt, opened the door and went inside, turned, and tore the door off its hinges.

I destroyed every book, story, poem, photograph, letter and object I'd given her, even the little things, and when I left I felt good. I went to an anonymous bar, and closed the place.

The next day there was a soft tapping on my door, and knowing who it was, but in spite of my hangover still angry, although rather ashamed of myself, I opened the door and there she was. I had never seen her so angry.

The blood had drained from her face, and her eyes were bloodshot from weeping. Her lips were puffed as was the skin around her eyes, but her lower lip was scratched and almost punctured from her having bitten on it.

Her chest heaved as she tried to find the words, and we stood there, looking at each other. I knew how deeply I'd hurt her, but still, I was angry. I said,

"Come on in."

She did, I closed the door and we sat at the table in my horrible little kitchenette. I made tea for us, but she hardly touched hers. Then she said,

"Everything. You destroyed everything I—had and loved of you," and she began to cry. She put her head in her hands and wept as her shoulders shuddered and I grit my teeth. Then she looked up, angry and hurt, tears running down her face,

"And you frightened me. I didn't know who had done it, who *could* have done *that*, and then I realized it was you. I couldn't understand why, *why!* and I couldn't sleep, there was no door, the place was a mess—"

"I know," I said.

Her eyebrows went up, tears welled anew in her eyes and her whole expression pleaded with me: "Can't I have my friends?"

She knew, and the wave of fury rose again in me, but I kept control. "Don't you know," I said, "that it was because of your friends that you lost me? I moved out because of your friend, and you were happy for yourself, and sorry to see me go, a little. I finished my novel, it was accepted and you were happy for me, from a distance. I signed and sent you a copy of the book and you were happy for both of us, please let me finish, and I invited you to the publication party and I never heard a word. Were you happy? yes you were, and I know you Alicia, and what has me bothered is this thing about *distance*. You have to be with me to love me, and when I'm not there you don't oh you do of course, but not actually."

"What publication party?"

"I sent you an announcement, over a month ago."

"Well I didn't get it!" she cried, wiping her eyes.

I rose from the table, went into my so-called study, opened a drawer in my desk and took out some extras, returned with an announcement and showed it to her, envelope and all. This is what it looked like, I said.

"Oh," she said, in a little voice, "that."

"Yes," I nodded. "You were glad when I moved out, weren't you. Tell the truth."

She lowered her head, and nodded. "Yes," she admitted, and then she looked up: "But I didn't know what to do. Lucky! I'd gotten used to you, it hadn't happened before, and I didn't know what was going to happen, and after Andrea left, I—"

"Andrea left? When?" Andrea had been the woman friend.

"Oh, a few weeks after you did."

"And you didn't tell me?"

"Lucky! Can't you understand?"

"Yes Goddamnit, I understand!" I said, savagely, "Of *course* I do, but can't *you* understand how *I* felt? Shall I answer for you? No. You couldn't, or at least you wouldn't. You didn't."

"It's true," she admitted. "I—inwardly I did, and I knew how hurt you were, but, I I didn't want to. Nobody's ever made any difference to me."

"I know," I said, tenderly, and looked at her, thinking of the things I had destroyed that she had loved of me, even the little things, like the warm notes, ticket stubs to plays, movies, ballgames, and the swizel sticks, curiously colored marbles, pins, and the tiny flowers, and wondering how it had gotten started, way back then.

110

"Except you," she said, "and I didn't know what to do."

I knew I'd mattered. "I know," I said, which didn't lessen her dilemma. Again she wiped her eyes, and looking up, sipped her cool tea, and said the building super put a new door on this morning, and after she had gotten new locks, he had installed them, she had a set of keys made, and had missed work, her boss was furious because they couldn't get a substitute on such short notice, so she took the day off. I sat there like a white toad, and she stood up, woebegone and hurt, and said goodbye.

"Let me take you home in a cab?" I asked.

"No," she said. "There's nothing you can do."

"Not if you won't let me," I said.

She turned to go toward the doorway, and then turned back, and shouted:

"HOW COULD YOU DO THAT TO ME!"

I stood up and went to her. "Because I was really angry, and still am."

"Yes," she said, "I know, but *that*, to *me?*"

Yet she knew. "You know," I said. "I didn't know how to tell you."

"You're such a baby, a *baby*," she said, angrily.

"Because I let you know how I felt, and how angry I was?"

She pulled a tissue from her bag and wiped her eyes, blew her nose, and looked square in my eyes. Her eyes were absolutely haunted.

"Goodbye, Lucky," she said, firmly, and walked out of my kitchenette, through the living room and out the door into the hall. The door closed softly, and the lock clicked. I stood there, and listened to the echo of that click. Not an echo, really, but the sound great carpenters know when they hit the nailhead squarely.

A year or so later I was at my typewriter writing letters and waiting for my Jency to come home and make

111

salad so I could make supper, and hearing the tapping at my door, I rose quickly, and because I was hungry, I opened the door ready to take the bag of vegetables from her arms, and my heart stood still.

"Come on in," I said, finally.

"Okay," she smiled, and came in, looked around, and then looked at me.

"I just read your novel again Lucky, it's wonderful."

She was wearing a white silk blouse and a blue and green paisley scarf at her throat under a tan chamois jacket which was open, and belt dangling. I recognized the bluejeans, the ones with the polka dot patch on the bottom.

Her feet were bare in blue yachting sneakers, and she wore her auburn hair in pigtails.

"Like some tea?" I asked.

She smiled, and nodded. Her face was wide open and her eyes were bright, and friendly.

We sat at the table in my kitchenette and I made tea. As I served it, she said she had something to tell me. She bit her lip.

"My father died last night. I'm going home tonight, and I'm going to stay with mother for a while."

"If you stay longer than two weeks you'll stay for ten years," I said.

She thought about that.

"Alicia," I said, "stay with her a few days, and then come back. Your life is here, not there. You won't help her by staying too long anyway, she'll need to adjust to herself by herself, and you can always go back to visit. You can help her more from this end than by being there. This is the true distance," I said.

The one she'd feared to put between her mother, and put between herself and everybody else.

"I see," she said. "You're right, again, Lucky, but I, feel, as, if, I must."

"Not completely, though."

"Never completely! Oh don't!" she cried. "Please, I've got—I must get myself together, and I can't do it here! You know that—you know me!"

"Why can't you do it here?" I asked, knowing she didn't want to.

"But how?" she pleaded. "Will you help me?"

I nodded. "You know I will."

She pursed her lips, lowered her head and fiddled with the buckle on the belt to her jacket, and sighed, saying, "I'm going to go home tonight anyway."

I said okay and she asked me if I'd help her with her luggage.

I said, Luggage? "What luggage?"

Then I said, "Oh yes, I see, you want me to help you."

She nodded, avoiding my eyes.

"Will you write me?" I asked.

She looked up, and beamed, her face and eyes radiant, and nodded. So I said I'd help her, and I did. I got her luggage into a cab for her (she had sold her apartment, and left the furniture behind, even the rocking chair), and told her that the guys at the cross-Metropolitan airline terminal would take care of it from there.

I closed the cab door after she'd gotten in, and she rolled down the window and our eyes met. I leaned forward and we kissed goodbye, and eleven years later I got the phone call from her telling me she was going overseas. Her mother had died, and she wanted to get out of the country, she said, unconsciously—once again—creating distance, and when she came through, I met her at the airport and we spent a couple of hours together on the lay-over.

Yet all the while, she had written. Not often, but often enough, and I had written back. And since she's been overseas, we've kept in touch, too.

It was nine years ago that she and I spent those couple of hours together, in the airport, and whenever I get a letter from her, a lot of it always comes back, and I often stand and gaze at that photo of her, with her wonderful open face and bright eyes, and her smile. The reason she's looking up, in the photo, is because she was seated at her table, and just before the photographer took the picture, I'd come forward, and she glanced up at me and made a big grin. I remember that afternoon, too, because every once in a while she'd tease me about our ages. She was born three months and two days before me, and thus, she being older than I was far more wise, and far more into the ways of the world than I, and in fact everything *generally* more than I, at which I laughed no end, which delighted her, and I remember that day the photo was taken, she'd been teasing me again, and suddenly I think of her as I've always thought of her, and always from the beginning, because there was a letter she wrote, just after her mother died, when Alicia Peabody told me her whole life story. It was a long letter, and as I glance into my memory it was, on the first day of next month, forty five years ago, that her life began.

Adieu

Blaze said, as I sipped the cold vodka, I saw Sandy last night (Sandy an old flame of his).

Yeah? I said. You were out last night?

Yes, he said, wearily. Dotty and I um visited with Mario and Helen and afterwards I came here. Dotty didn't want to come, I don't know why (ha ha), nor do I know why even I came, can you figure it out and do you think it was because I was drunk?

Perhaps, I said.

I thought so, he said. Most unusual for me, or us, to be out at night.

I agreed that was true, and I asked, sensing something

he might be holding back—Did you go to that after hours joint, what's the name again?

The Diamond Cafe, Blaze whispered.

We both laughed, and I sipped, as he sat hunched over.

The Diamond Cafe was an after hours joint owned by the Mafia, and it stayed open until the legal bars opened, when it closed. But before the legal bars opened, different people stopped in for a fast one to begin their day. Truck drivers, mailmen, cops, poets and artists and assorted tough guys. Food isn't served at The Diamond Cafe, nor do they offer any mixers besides water. At least they didn't in the old days. It was beer, whiskey, Scotch, and water. Before Blaze and Dotty had gotten married, and also Audrey and me, Blaze and I used to go there fairly often. That was when we went out at nights, which we rarely do, anymore.

The bartender's name was Ski. He was also the manager and the waiter, in fact he was the only one there besides the customers, every night. It was a very small place, and of course the business didn't draw a landoffice crowd, always a few guys who drank from four in the morning when it opened until eight o'clock—four hours later—when the legal bars opened, so Ski's hours were good, and the work wasn't hard. But Ski had died, and with his death went my interest in The Diamond Cafe.

He had been a small thin, even gaunt, but very tough, yet warm man, and always soft spoken, and for some reason he took a liking to me. It goes without saying there was never any trouble in The Diamond Cafe. Ski didn't get his nickname because it was the last syllable in his surname, nor because he enjoyed the sport, but because of the Polish men with whom he had dealt, as Blaze would say, in a rather final way. Thus there was a chill in the place, yet in his small ruthless body, Ski lent a certain mad humor to it all, and it was he who made the joint what it was, to me anyway, although I never went there sober, and was generally in fact always very drunk and in the mood to go down into the Labyrinth and see Ski. I liked him, and one day I'll tell you why. It involves (my story does), a tall airline stewardess of whom I was once very fond, and Ski's traditional respect for women.

Well well, I said. *The Diamond Cafe.* Has the place changed.

You have some sense of humor, Blaze said.

Did you take Sandy with you?

I did, he said.

Did she like it?

Yes.

Was Charley Lowery there?

No, and we all missed his singing.

I'll bet, I laughed. Remember how Ski let him sing?

I do, but, Blaze said, Ski was the only one who didn't mind if Charley sang loud. That was the point, not just the singing.

That's right, I said. Ski liked it, even. It reminded him of the college he never went to, probably. How's Sandy?

Lovely as always, Blaze said. In fact more so. He took a sip, a small sip, of his drink, which was pretty near all water, and rather suddenly he sagged, and was exhausted. When he spoke, his words were slurred. Yet he spoke slowly, and carefully.

As you know, he began, I haven't seen her in years, and last night, well, Lucky, I fell in love with her all over again. She's looking, as you would say, great. She still has those level serious eyes, and the way she walks hasn't changed either. She is, I think, involved with the film world. My memory is a little off today, so forgive me.

You're forgiven, I said. Go on.

Oh well, she asked me how I was, and I said Me? and made a vague wave (which he did): "There's no news."

Coming from you, Sandy had said, that's news in

itself, she, she with her warm and honest heart, like Debbie waiting tables at the tailend of the decade when I and the rest of us stared straight out into oblivion and Debbie occasionally sat with me when she took breaks and oh, *Lucky* you remember, *you* were there with us, oh and *boy* we had seen and read and heard the news that day, about a lucky man who made the grade in Southeast Asia, in napalm, gunfire, helicopters and the screaming.

And she remembered, too. And asked me, Blaze reported, How was I doing, *really*. Really? and I told her I will have finished two new major collections of poetry by year's end, and it's great to see you—

But sensing something change in (the adverb) way he said *really*, I turned in my seat, away from my drunken friend, as he finished his sentence—

again. Really.

In a premonition I gazed across the restaurant.

"Look Blaze!" I cried. "There's Asa! She's back!"

Blaze turned and peered across the floor, adjusting his vision, until he saw as I did, Asa, sitting in a booth with another man. They were having a late lunch.

Who's the fella? I wondered aloud.

I—don't—know, Blaze murmured, but I've seen him around. He's a writer with a certain reputation, one could say and to hell with him. Did you know I'll be fifty years old, quite soon?

But then Blaze fell silent.

Asa looked wonderful, and I wondered where she'd gotten so tan—on the Alps, of course.

The fellow with her had grey hair, and like myself was in jeans and an orange sweatshirt, and worn sneakers without socks. Some men gossip about each other. I—never do. But he was speaking to her in an animated fashion, using his right hand.

She seemed to be enjoying it, in fact they seemed to be enjoying themselves, and it was a pleasure to see her happy, although I was and I admit it, jealous.

He had an expression, speaking to her, of sheer enthusiasm, he was looking directly and intently at her, completely absorbed by his story, or whatever story he was telling her, no doubt a tall one, and he had that smile that in a fraction was going to burst into a grin and then a hearty laugh. The kind that follows a punchline, and he was quite clearly the kind of man that enjoys his own jokes, which is exactly what happened, and they sat there, facing each other laughing.

"Want another drink?" he asked her.

"No," she said, "I've got to get home, am just in, you know, and the flight was a long one."

"Okay," he said, and as they had finished their lunch, he stood up as the waitress crossed over, and paid her, left a tip on the table and as she began to put on her raincoat, he at first went to help her, but then didn't, so he put on his own coat as she did hers and he then had the nerve to straighten the back of her collar. For which she *thanked* him, and *smiled* to him! I saw what was in his eyes, that rascal.

"ASA!" Blaze yelled, nearly falling off the barstool. I held him!

She turned and waved to us, saying she *really* had to run, she'd just gotten back! Would we call her soon? She'd love to see us!

We waved cheerfully and agreed we would, oh we waved adieu as she, to my intense irritation, put her arm through his, and they walked out the front door. I know what her arm feels like, and let me tell ya it feels good!

119

Blaze cursed, and we glumly turned to our drinks. Frank drifted down the bar to us, and pointed to where Asa had been sitting.

"I think that fella left something, would you get it Lucky? I'll keep it here in case he comes back."

"Who is he?" I asked.

I thought you'd know, Frank said, and told us.

That's it! Blaze exclaimed. I knew it! Well, well! I'm sorry I didn't meet him.

I am too, I said, for I knew his work, and Blaze and I crossed the room and picked up an envelope, which had the writer's name and address on it.

We opened it, and looked inside. There were galley sheets for what looked like a novel, so we took them out and unfolded them, and sure enough, that's what it was! Galley sheets for a novel, and when we looked at the title, we gasped! and Blaze said, He could have called it Strawberry Fields, and I laughed as Blaze remarked it meant the end.

The end? I asked.

Yes, Blaze said, and staggered a little.

"Why don't you take it back to him," Frank suggested, "and meet him while you're at it. He only lives a block or so from here."

Blaze and I looked at each other.

We will go quietly, and we shall return, Frank, Blaze said, so we finished our drinks, and as Blaze had come more awake, and to any person who cared to notice, he appeared to be sober, so quietly, quietly, and really. Quietly, we left the bar.

They returned the envelope with the galleys inside, to me.

They walked through the glass doors, and handed it to me. I took it and thanked them. But they were mute, and shy. I had left it for them to give back to me. It is after all, meant to be.

120

"You'll return and talk again," I said, pleasantly.

They smiled, as I wrote, which they had read, the way they should smile: in a sad way.

They gestured farewell, and in their step, backed out of the doors, fading as they went.

It was raining outside. Hard.

Their images faded, became transparent, and then disappeared.

Outside my door the sidewalk was empty. Lucky and Blaze and Bugs and Flap, and the other selves and voices —all were gone from the street and the traffic, in the pouring rain.

Very strange.

Printed September 1977 in Santa Barbara & Ann Arbor
for the Black Sparrow Press by Mackintosh and Young
& Edwards Brothers Inc. Design by Barbara Martin.
Cover collage by Fielding Dawson. This edition is
published in paper wrappers; there are 250 hardcover
copies numbered & signed by the author; & 26 lettered
copies handbound in boards by Earle Gray each with
an original drawing by Fielding Dawson.

Photo: Ray Hartman

. . . one of the most original of prose writers . . . he approaches the page as an energy field, filling it with action the same way Kline used to fill his canvases. Few writers of prose have ever gotten so close to the *facts* of life: Dawson is Henry James in reverse; he catches those moments of intense perception, sees into the mystery of things, but does so with the brevity of an imagist poet . . .

F. Whitney Jones
St. Andrews Review, 1977